KU-158-151

# BLOOD ON THE DRAGON

A mysterious murder cult . . . a man who has no identity . . . an ancient hidden temple in the remote hills of China . . . And mixed with these ingredients is the brutal story of the Purple Dragon Tong and the man who knows too much . . . While in *Sinister Honeymoon,* two newlyweds have their celebrations interrupted by a vampire! Can they find a way to escape the perils they face before it's too late? Two stories of murder, mystery and the supernatural by Norman Firth.

*Books by Norman Firth*
*in the Linford Mystery Library:*

WHEN SHALL I SLEEP AGAIN?
CONCERTO FOR FEAR
THE LITTLE GREY MAN
THE MODEL MURDERS
FIND THE LADY

# NORMAN FIRTH

◆

# BLOOD ON THE DRAGON

*Complete and Unabridged*

**LINFORD**
*Leicester*

First published in Great Britain

First Linford Edition
published 2015

Copyright © 1946 by Norman Firth
Copyright © 2014 by Sheila Ings
All rights reserved

A catalogue record for this book is available
from the British Library.

ISBN 978–1–4448–2483–4

Published by
F. A. Thorpe (Publishing)
Anstey, Leicestershire

Set by Words & Graphics Ltd.
Anstey, Leicestershire
Printed and bound in Great Britain by
T. J. International Ltd., Padstow, Cornwall

This book is printed on acid-free paper

KENT
ARTS & LIBRARIES

# Contents

# Blood on the Dragon

# 1

## The Man Who Knew Himself

On the southern banks of the Wei Ho River in China, halfway between Tsin-Ling and Tsin-Chow, stands the small town of Liang-Sin.

On a chilly March night, while the river rolled sluggishly down to the Yellow Sea hundreds of miles away, a young American sat in a squalid office in Liang-Sin, listening intently to the half-whispered words of the emaciated Chinaman who stood in front of his desk, jabbering in the high-pitched vernacular of the Chinese labourer. While he listened to the intriguing story the man told him, not two hundred miles away the massed hordes of the Japanese armies prepared for their next push which was to take them to Tsin-Chow and beyond. But here, in this small office building which he had rented for a time, they were forgotten in the story of incredible villainy and treachery which the thin Chinaman was relating to him. From time to time he made notes on a small pad before him, but the majority of the names mentioned by his companion went into the files of his retentive memory.

' . . . and now that you know all,' finished the speaker, 'pay me the money you promised and permit me to go with haste! Soon they will find me, and then . . . ' He left the sentence unspoken, but the look of fear in his eyes finished it for him.

The young man nodded, and replying in Chinese himself, handed his companion an agreed sum of money. Scarcely waiting to voice his thanks and farewell, the Chinaman turned towards the door, then froze where he stood.

There was a shadow on the frosted glass! It was the figure of a gigantic semi-naked man, facing sideways. His head, massively proportioned, could be seen in profile, and revealed the complete lack of hair save for the short, thick pigtail which rested down his unclothed back.

He was motionless, his shadow rendered grotesque by the effect of the dim light burning above his head.

The Chinaman who had been speaking shrank against the desk in an agony of apprehension. His eyes, terrified and appealing, moved towards the face of the young American, who also sat silent, staring at the apparition outlined on the frosted glass of the door.

'God!' he suddenly exploded. 'What the hell's that?'

'Chala!' stammered the Chinaman, his voice low and trembling. 'Chala has come for me — and now that you know he will take you, also!'

'Not if I can help it,' said the American grimly. 'Let's get that door locked, Lin See, before he comes through it. Then we may be able to get out of the window.'

He rose to his feet and took a key from his pocket, but he was too late. Before he had taken a step the handle of the door began to turn slowly . . . The shadow on the door moved forward until it filled the glass like an evil phantasm of doom . . . The door was swung silently inwards.

5

The man on the threshold caused even the strong-nerved American man to gasp. He was tall, so tall that to enter the room he had to stoop under the fanlight. His shoulders, naked and writhing with corded muscles, filled the doorway; his round, hairless yellow skull glittered in the lamplight. A broad, flat nose with distended nostrils overhung his wide, cavernous mouth which housed a double row of black and putrid teeth. Hidden in the fleshy folds of his face, two holes denoted his eye sockets, but only one flaring eye was visible; the other appeared to have been torn out in some manner, and the fleshy red hole which resulted sickened the American. He advanced into the room without speaking, and with him advanced two more Chinese, equally repulsive in a smaller way.

'What the hell do *you* want?' snapped the American; then, realizing that the newcomers would not understand his language, he repeated the question in the vernacular.

The two smaller men had moved towards the shrinking man by the desk, and had taken a firm hold of him. Now one of them spoke. 'We regret the intrusion,' he said, 'but our leaders are of the opinion that our brother, Lin See, has been telling you that which it is not good for men to know!'

'I told them nothing — *nothing*,' babbled Lin See. 'I swear by my sacred ancestors that I have spoken of the Purple Dragon Tong to no one . . . '

'You lie,' hissed the other. 'We heard all you said to this man — oh, yes, we followed you here. You were incompetent — you failed to do the task which was entrusted to you — and you thought that you could obtain money from this man by exposing our society and then fleeing to some other city where our vengeance could not reach you. You should know better than that, brother Lin See! As for swearing by your sacred ancestors — well you will be able to answer to them personally for that, for shortly you will be joining them!'

'Come,' snapped the third man, 'we have wasted enough time — secure the American gentleman, Chala!'

The young American sucked his breath in sharply as the giant Chinaman started towards him. Suddenly his hands flew to the right-hand drawer of the desk where he kept a revolver, but the giant divined his intention and, moving with remarkable speed and agility, hurled himself round the desk, hands outstretched.

One tremendous hand seized the American's throat; the other swung back to deliver a jarring blow. But before it could land, the American's heavy shoe kicked hard into the giant's abdomen, just above his loincloth.

'Ugh!' rasped the monstrosity, then with fury blazing from his one good eye, he tightened his grasp on his adversary's throat and began to squeeze.

Weak and helpless in the grip of Chala, the American kicked and struggled feebly, but those giant hands about his windpipe slowly, inexorably, cut off his supply of air. Dimly he could see that one blazing eye, glaring from an otherwise vacuous face. There was something unbelievably horrible in the way the man was killing him; his face never changed as his hands tightened. It remained blank, heavy, idiotic, almost like the face of a small child who is tearing the wings from a butterfly. He felt the vomit coming up from his stomach, felt it surge towards his throat, and stop where the throat had been closed together. He sagged. Through his glazing eyes he could see a round, red piece of flesh hanging from his face; his stomach turned again as he realized that it was his own tongue!

The office began to spin, faster and faster, until it was like a blurred mass rushing past his head. In the middle of the blur a dark pit commenced to open ... Headlong, he plunged towards it.

As if from a great distance he heard a voice: 'That's enough, Chala ... ' And then, more sharply: 'I said that's enough! If you kill this man you will have to answer to the Master!'

The choking grip around the American's throat relaxed. Like an empty sack he was flung across the giant's shoulder. He had the sensation of being carried swiftly from the room, down the stairs.

As the fresh air hit him, he opened his

eyes again. Still only half-conscious, he gazed up at the clear, pale moon which hung in the ebony sky above him. He thought irrelevantly, 'Nice night for bombers!' Then he tried to distinguish the dark streets through which he was being carried, but found it was hopeless.

His mind, functioning more clearly now, began to revolve about a plan of escape. He was weaponless, helpless in the grasp of the leviathan, Chala. He knew he was being rushed to death — possibly horrible, lingering death, as was the small Chinaman who had said too much to him.

He was aware that his presence in Liang-Sin would have been frowned on by the authorities, but certain rumours he had heard had convinced him it would be worthwhile to sneak into the town to see if he could get to the bottom of the mystery which surrounded the old quarter of it. And he had — only to put his foot into a viper's nest!

It was certain death for him, he knew that. He knew too much; could have exposed too many eminent townsfolk in their true colours. He knew everything!

His gently moving hand encountered the shape of a penknife in his jacket pocket; his heart raced as he eased it out and opened the large blade. At any rate, it was worth a try. He struck hard at the heavily muscled back beneath him. There was a cry of rage and pain; then he was whirled round, his head cannoned into a wall, and he plunged abruptly into that black pit . . .

# 2

## The Cellar of the Purple Dragon

It might have been centuries, or merely minutes, that he felt himself floating in a black eternity. But gradually his senses returned; slowly the shrill whining in his head ceased and he opened his eyes and gazed about him.

He was in what appeared to be a cellar. A flight of wooden steps led downwards to a floor composed of hard-trodden dirt. The walls were of heavy timber, and the place was illuminated by six Chinese lanterns fashioned in the shape of the head of a dragon and painted purple. Their glow cast a strange and sinister radiance over the rest of the cellar.

The wooden walls were painted: each wall bore a mural of part of a dragon, outlined against a background of green, rotting putrescence. Taking the four walls together, the artist had managed to convey the impression of a dragon being coiled round the entire room and its occupants — it was as if the walls were glass, and the dragon encircled them. The head — with gaping, open jaws — was painted on the wall directly facing him, hardly five yards distant.

Immediately below the head rested a rough wooden altar with ominous stains down the sides. On top of this was a claw-like metal instrument. Suspended behind the altar was Lin See, who had played the traitor to his Tong. His mouth lolled open in fear and dread; his arms were drawn over his head and secured to a beam of wood running across the ceiling. Near to him stood the ugly Chala, his features still vague and stupid.

On a number of seats along the left-hand wall sat eight men; there were the two who had been with Chala previously, and six more of the same type. They were attired in European clothing, and were obviously men of some importance in Liang-Sin. Only one of them stood out to any extent; he was a tall, thin man with a venerable appearance which was belied by his two thin, bloodless lips, the emblems of sadism and cruelty.

The American weighed up his own position; he was neither gagged nor bound, and glancing up the steps towards the closed door, he saw why. For there was a brawny guard there, armed with a long, curved sword. No chance of escape up there!

The most distinguished-looking of the Chinamen raised his sleeve and glanced at the watch round his wrist. 'Let us array ourselves in our ceremonial robes,' he said. 'The Master will be here soon!'

The American watched them as all except Chala and the guard took their weirdly embroidered robes from a number of hooks on the wall. When they had donned them they were transformed from civilized men into the likeness of ancient, forgotten priests of some Chinese legend. On their heads they slipped black skull caps, and the transformation was complete.

Hardly had they completed this ritual than there was a sharp knock on the door above. It was repeated eight times at

14

regular intervals, and the guard swiftly shot the bolt and admitted a newcomer. He descended the steps and passed within a few feet of the American without looking at him even. And the American was aware of a shock of surprise as he realized the man was a European.

From the attitude of the others it was clear that this man was the Master; and the American, from his first words, placed him as probably English.

'I see that you have caught them both,' he exclaimed, getting into a ceremonial robe like the rest. 'Good work! And now we must teach them that it does not pay to interfere with the workings of our society. Chala!'

The giant turned his great head towards the Master, licking his blubbery lips.

'I know you *like* this sort of thing,' said the Master, smiling, 'so I shall leave it to you to punish Lin See. We will attend to him first — that will give our American guest an idea of the fate which is in store for him.'

Chala grinned, displaying his corrupt

teeth. He picked up the three-clawed metal instrument from the altar and advanced towards the squirming Lin See, who was slobbering crazily.

'His eyes first,' said the Master unemotionally. 'That he may not see things which he cannot hold his tongue about!'

The American watched in fascinated horror; the metal claw in the hands of Chala darted forward and scooped at one of Lin See's protruding eyeballs ... A ghastly shriek rent the air, then the detached eye was ripped away and thrown to the floor.

Shriek after shriek strained from Lin See's drooling lips. His body jerked and heaved frantically, his remaining eye rolling madly in his skull.

'Gag him,' snapped the Master, 'lest his screams bring someone down here.'

As they gagged the tortured Lin See, the American came from his seat, madly. He had stood all he could; all he meant to stand. He hurled himself across the floor and hit Chala just below the knees. But before he could move further, six pairs of hands gripped him; six Chinese dragged him struggling towards the rough bench he had been seated on. And then a hand sought a vulnerable spot at the base of his neck, pressed hard and half-paralyzed him, so that he dare not move.

'Continue,' said the Master complacently.

Chala grinned and did so.

Once again the claw forked out, and Lin See's remaining eye was torn from its socket. His shrieks penetrated even through the gag; but they were muffled, indistinct. He hung there, sightless and agonized, and the American was praying that he would faint and be spared any further agony. But Lin See had a tough constitution; he did not faint. His body continued to jerk and jump wildly.

'Now his *tongue* that he may not talk,' grated the Master.

The tortured man's mouth was forced open, and the claw was driven deep into the roots of the tongue. With a strong motion, Chala ripped it from the throat. Hastily the gag was stuffed back into Lin See's maltreated, bloody maw.

Chala then looked questioningly at the Master, who waved him to one side. He himself walked over to the jerking figure; he turned round and said: 'Take the sword, Chala — strike off his *legs*!'

The American strove to look away, but some strange fascination dragged his gaze back to the brutal scene. He watched Lin See's legs fall dully to the floor; saw the remaining stumps, bleeding profusely. He tried to curse, but the agonizing grip on his neck prevented him from speaking.

His stomach swivelled over again, and this time he was violently sick.

'Cut him down,' rapped the Master. So they did. They cut Lin See down by the simple expedient of hacking away his arms at the elbows. The bloody trunk which had been a man lay there, twitching and jumping. The master nodded, and Chala brought the sword swishing down onto Lin See's gory neck. It was over!

But as they all stood motionless for a moment, gazing at the mess on the floor, the American, in a desperate mood, acted. His bunched fist swept up and cannoned into the chin of the man holding his neck.

And before any of them could move he was up the stairs and had kicked out at the guard on the door. The guard was taken by surprise; his sword swung futilely in a circle, under which the young American dodged easily. He was seized by the arms and thrown sprawling over the rail, to thud on the floor ten feet below. Then the door was open, and the captive was running for his life along the narrow, deserted thoroughfares.

Far behind him he could hear the rapid patter of light sandals; his own heavy shoes, clattering along, gave his direction away in the deserted street.

He suddenly became aware of the loud droning sound from the blackness of the sky. He knew now why the streets were empty: bombers! Still his flying feet carried him on, seeking safety. And still he could hear the relentless patter of his pursuers' feet.

Then the bombs began to come whining down, filling his ears with a terrifying cacophony of sound . . . exploding, erupting, blasting, maiming innocent women and children. The night was lurid with the orange glare of bursting high explosives. The moon was blotted out by a curtain of flying dust motes. And still the bombers droned overhead, sending their cargo of whistling death on the defenceless city. But now he could no longer hear the noise of his pursuers. He paused to listen — and in that instant heard the sound of a thousand banshees screaming down towards him. Instinctively he threw himself flat, but the bursting bomb picked him up and hurled him with mighty hands into the air . . .

# 3

## The Man Who Forgot Himself

In a small, hastily erected hospital, one morning in the month of September 1945, a man struggled back to consciousness. A Chinese nurse clad in immaculate white noticed his first slight flickering movements; noticed also his semi-opened eyes. She immediately went for the sole doctor in the place.

When the patient fully recovered, the doctor was sitting on a chair by his bedside, gazing at him intently. The patient's eyes rested on the light lemon complexion of the medical man, then shifted to his white smock and trousers. He raised a hand wearily and passed it across his brow. His questing eyes took in other details of the low-roofed, light-wood building; the other patients Chinese, all of them.

'I am pleased to see that you have recovered,' said the doctor in perfect

English, and the man had no difficulty in knowing what he said.

'What — happened?' His words came haltingly, uncertainly.

The doctor smiled and said, 'I'm afraid what I have to say will be rather a shock to you — do you think you are well enough to hear it?'

The patient shrugged impatiently. 'I feel quite well.'

'Very well.' The doctor fumbled in his white pocket and offered the patient a cigarette. The patient took it with nodded thanks.

'You were bombed,' the doctor informed him gravely. 'They brought you in here in a very bad state. You suffered a head injury which might easily have proved fatal — in fact, for some time I despaired for your life altogether. Fortunately, with the help of my nurse we pulled you through. Do you want me to go on?'

The man nodded. The doctor leaned forward with his elbows on the bed. He looked very worn, very tired, although he could not have been more than thirty years of age. He said, 'You have lain here unconscious for almost six months. We have operated on you eight times to endeavour to remove the splinters of bone which pressed on your brain. We have fed you through a tube, since you lacked the ability to swallow. Our last trepan was performed three days ago, and seemingly it has proved successful.'

The man in the bed took all this in, in silence. Finally he nodded slowly. He said, 'I guess I owe you my life, Doctor. But my memory isn't functioning too well so far. I mean, maybe you know — er, who I am? I can't seem to recall my name — or what I was doing when I was bombed. Possibly you discovered some means of identification on me . . . did you?'

The doctor shook his head. 'I was afraid of this complication,' he murmured. 'And it is something about which I can do nothing. No, there was no means of identifying you. The blast of the explosive ripped every shred of clothing from you . . . you were carried here naked.'

'But — surely — surely there must be

some clue. How about the people who brought me here?'

'Labourers from the fields — they brought you in along with their own dead and wounded. The only thing I could tell was that you belonged to one of the white races — you might have been French, Russian, English, American. Do any of those names convey anything to you?'

'I — I'm afraid not. No, nothing.'

'I think we can reasonably assume that English is your national language, since it is the first you spoke. Can you speak any other?'

The man who had forgotten himself strained his memory. Then he spoke a phrase in reasonably good Chinese. The doctor nodded.

'You do not speak my language with the correct accent,' he stated. 'But in either case it is obvious that you are certainly not of our race. Is that the only other language you know?'

After a short pause, the patient said it was.

'Then I think we may take it for granted that you are either English,

Canadian or American. I doubt if you are Australian — there is a certain twang about the speech of most Australians which renders them instantly recognizable. I don't suppose you remember what you were doing here?'

'I don't. I don't even know where *here* is.'

'You are in Liang-Sin,' the doctor informed him. 'A small town midway between Tsin-Chow and Tsin-Ling, on the banks of the River Wei Ho. That tells you nothing? No? Perhaps if I mention the war with Japan you will remember?'

'War? Japan? No, I guess not. Was that how I came to be bombed?'

'It was. Fortunately, with the aid of England, America and Russia, Japan has now declared herself defeated. The war ended last month.'

The patient turned his head away and stared down the ward. He said, 'Hell, I must find out who I am! But how?'

'I have made numerous enquiries,' the doctor informed him. 'But I have discovered nothing. As a matter of fact, there were no white people living in

Liang-Sin when the raid in which you were injured occurred. It is a mystery where you came from, seemingly.' He noticed the harassed look which had crept into the stranger's eyes. He said, 'Anyhow, suppose you just get some more sleep and leave it for now. Your memory may return when you feel stronger.'

But it was a long time before the patient could sleep. For hours he lay restlessly, frantically racking his blank brain for some sign of his past existence. It was useless, though. One thing, and one thing only could he remember dimly, and it sounded silly to him. It was a phrase; just that, and nothing more. It was: 'the Purple Dragon'.

★　★　★

Within a month he was strong and well again, and had learned how to walk anew. The scars of his head operations were healed, scarcely noticeable beneath his crisp, wavy dark hair. His face, although a little pale from his long confinement in the hospital, was yet determined-looking and handsome. He had in no way wasted, as do some hospital cases. Rather, the rest had done him good, and he felt refreshed and more settled in his mind. But still his identity eluded him.

During the last two weeks he helped the doctor and nurse with the rest of the patients. Looking at them, people who had been hopelessly maimed by bomb attacks, he began to thank his stars that nothing more serious than loss of memory had befallen him. And yet, the problem of his missing life weighed heavily on him. He was determined to find just who he was and what he was.

He found the young Chinese doctor a congenial companion; Dr. Lo Wond had taken his degrees in medicine and surgery at an American university, and each time the doctor spoke of America the patient felt a strange sense of longing, wistfulness. So strong a feeling that he decided he must be American — for when England or any other country was mentioned, he felt no reaction.

At last came the day when he could stay no longer. Although the doctor appreciated his help, the hospital being sadly understaffed, his bed was urgently needed for one of the victims of a wave of cholera which was sweeping the country.

'Doctor,' he said, as he stood outside the door shaking hands with that worthy, 'you deserve a medal for all you are doing here! And thanks for the suit and the dough you lent me — as soon as I find out who the devil I really am, I'll repay you.'

'My humble gifts are as nothing,' said Lo Wond, smiling. 'Please forget them. But are you sure you would not rather journey to the American Embassy at Chung-King, and see if they can trace your lineage?'

The American shook his head decidedly. 'Nope! I've got a feeling that somewhere in this town I'll find someone who knows me, and who can put me straight. There must be someone. A guy doesn't just drop from nowhere without any previous life. Besides, there's that peculiar phrase that keeps running through my head — 'the Purple Dragon'. What in hell can that mean?'

'I have never heard of it,' said Lo Wond. 'Possibly you dreamed of a purple dragon in your delirium?'

Once again the American shook his head decidedly. 'I haven't. I feel certain that those two words tie in with my past life somehow. I'm determined to stay here until I find out why I ever came here in the first place, and what happened to me before I tried to buck a bomb!'

'Then if you are determined to stay, permit me to give you a letter to the only Englishman in Liang-Sin.'

'I understood you to say that there were no white men in Liang-Sin?' said the American, puzzled.

'I am sorry, my friend. I always forget the reverend. He is as much a part of the town as the river is. He is the missionary here, and has served this community well for over thirty years. He lives in quite a nice mission station on the outskirts of the town — until recently we were using it as an auxiliary hospital, but now that I am able to accommodate all the sick here, he will have plenty of room for you, should you desire to stay. I will write a short letter explaining your position to him — I know you will feel better with a confidante, and that you will find the Reverend Harper both a kind and helpful gentleman.'

The note was written, and after more goodbyes the American without a life began to follow the directions Lo Wond had given him for reaching the mission station.

He had turned out of the village and was walking along the riverbank when from round the bend of a building a girl on a bicycle suddenly appeared. She was coming straight towards him and, as she observed him standing blankly, unable to move to either side because of the river and the buildings, she wrenched desperately at the handlebars and smashed haphazardly into the flimsy wall of the nearest building.

# 4

## Diana

'Well!' exploded the girl. She lay amidst the wreckage of her bicycle, a tangle of arms and legs — and very shapely legs, the American couldn't help noticing. She was young, and she was a white girl. She was also exceedingly pretty, with that brand of prettiness which goes with fair, wavy hair and a suntanned skin. She was simply dressed in a white drill dress, which helped to accentuate the delightful curves of her tall figure more than any amount of slinky evening gowns would have done.

The man might have lost his memory, but he hadn't forgotten what a beautiful girl looked like; and his eyes smiled at her as he helped her from the ground. She stood up and he began to dust off her clothing, but she haughtily pushed his hand away and said, 'Thanks, but I can manage it myself!'

He lifted the sorry-looking wreckage of the bike and tried to straighten the twisted handlebars. The girl eyed him with some heat. She demanded, 'You awful chump! Fancy getting right in the way like that! Why on earth didn't you dodge?'

'Dodge?' exclaimed the American. 'Where could I dodge? What did you expect me to do — pitch myself into the river, or bust through the wall of this house?'

'Huh!' she snorted.

A small Chinaman attired in the native garb, and wearing thickly padded shoes, had emerged from the house which the girl had banged into. He stood with a mournful face, regarding the break in the flimsy wooden wall. He turned to the girl and said, 'It is you, gracious white sister!'

'Yes,' answered the girl in his own language. 'I am sorry I smashed into your honourable dwelling in such manner, Layosan.'

The Chinaman folded his hands in the sleeves of his tunic and smiled politely. 'It is nothing, little white sister,' he said, smiling. 'I am only too sorry that my humble home was in your way. I call down a thousand curses upon my wretched head, that I should have been the cause of your coming to grief! And yet, it is an honour for your illustrious self to come into contact with my meagre domicile.'

'The contact was a little too violent, O Layosan,' she said, smiling. 'However, I will send one of Uncle's servants along to help you effect the necessary repairs to your so-magnificent dwelling.'

The Chinaman bowed low and retreated again. The American, who had listened to the foregoing with an amused smile, said, 'They surely do like you around here, little white sister!'

'None of your cheek,' retorted the girl, but she smiled a little. She went on: 'I haven't seen you about here before . . . had no idea there were any Americans in the district. You are an American, aren't you?'

'I guess so,' he said with a smile. 'You see, I don't really know. I know it will sound funny to you, but I've no idea who I am or what I am. I recovered consciousness in hospital, and they told me I'd been bombed and had been unconscious for months. Apart from that I'm completely in a fog!'

'Oh,' said the girl, startled. 'Then you're the man whom Dr. Lo Wond operated on several times?'

'How did you know that?'

'Why, the doctor often comes along to the mission station, and he mentioned the matter to Uncle and me once or twice.'

'Then you're from the mission station?'

'Yes — I'm the Reverend Harper's niece, Diana. Uncle Jim is my only living relative. I came out here to him about two years ago, when my own father died in Shanghai. He was killed — the war, you know . . .'

The American saw the pain in her blue eyes and nodded quickly. 'I know — let's not talk about it. Let's talk about you, for example.'

'I'm sorry — I really must be carting this wrecked bike to the station.'

'You don't think I could let you do

that,' expostulated the American. 'Here, I'll take it.' He slung the wreck over his athletic shoulders, ignoring the girl's pleas that he wasn't well enough to do things like that. He said pleasantly, as they began to walk along the bank, 'I was coming along anyway. Dr. Lo Wond gave me a letter for your uncle, explaining all about me. I thought he hadn't mentioned my case to the Reverend?'

'Oh, he'd give you a note because Uncle's so absent-minded, you see. He has an awful job remembering anything.'

'I see. But the doctor never said that there was a pretty young lady at the station.'

She smiled. 'He wouldn't, of course. You see, although the doctor is awfully nice, he's really still a Chinaman at heart. I mean his Westernization is merely a veneer — inside he still holds the beliefs of his ancestors. And in those beliefs, women aren't important enough to count in life, except as a kind of foot-mat for the men!'

'He may be right at that,' said the American, grinning.

'Mr. — well, whoever you are — I think you're very rude!' said Diana, but her eyes twinkled.

They turned in at the gates of a wooden stockade and crossed a carefully tended garden. The station was a long hutment, with a veranda running the full length of the front of it. As they went up the steps, having dumped the bike at the gate, a stout but not short man rose from a wicker chair. He wore a pince-nez and a white drill suit. The jacket showed a marked tendency to sag, especially about the pockets, and it was by no means spotless. The trousers were concertinaed into deep creases, and gave the effect of a man about to jump. The shoes he wore were old tennis pumps, cut short at the toes to accommodate a choice selection of ripe bunions and corns. A worn, briar pipe drooped from one corner of his plump mouth, and a tobacco-stained moustache drooped above it. His nose was a blobby button, stuck on between two genial, if lazy, eyes, above which white, shaggy brows bristled outwards. His head was devoid of hair, except where his ears had their being. Here were two tufts, sticking out like a pair of flaps.

'Eh, what?' he mumbled amiably when the American had made himself known, and had handed him the letter from Lo Wond. 'Glad to have you, m'boy! Of course we can find room for you. Diana, get hold of that lazy scamp Ching and tell him to prepare the end room for our guest, Mr. — Hm! Mr. what? Can't have that! Must call you something. Suppose we call you Mr. — hmm! Mr. Green, eh? Just to be getting along with. And to make it less formal I'll refer to you as — Jack! How will that be?'

'Fine, Mr. Harper, fine!' They settled down in chairs, and a servant brought cooling drinks along. After a little desultory conversation, the new Jack Green said: 'Mr. Harper — have you ever heard of anything called . . . the Purple Dragon?'

# 5

## Danger in the Dark

The plump missionary raised his eye-
brows, but said nothing for some time.
Eventually the American, feeling that the
reverend had failed to hear him, repeated
the question.

Harper shook his sparsely covered head
slowly. He said, 'No, my boy, I haven't.
You know, here in China you are among a
people who, for the most part, exist amid
a welter of ancient customs, religions and
superstitions. I mean that there exist
many queer phrases; combinations of
words with very little real meaning behind
them. Possibly you heard some old legend
about a purple dragon before you were
injured, and it has stuck in your mind.'

'But that's hardly probable, sir, is it? I
mean I could hardly forget all about
myself, and yet remember words from a
casually told legend.'

'Stranger things have happened! Do you mean to say that you remember nothing besides those two words? Nothing whatever?'

Jack shook his head. 'Not a thing, sir.'

Diana, who had arranged for Jack's room and had returned to the veranda, broke in. 'Perhaps some of the local people would know something?'

Her uncle shook his head decidedly. 'I shouldn't go asking too many questions in the town. The Chinese tend to resent any prying into their beliefs or their way of life. They have formed their values from their long-dead ancestors, and what may seem to you a perfectly innocent question, to them would be an unforgivable intrusion. In thirty years I have learned to respect their peculiarities — their modes of greeting are almost exactly opposite to our own. Our conventional phrases would undoubtedly offend the Chinaman — yet he would consider it perfectly polite if you were to ask him how his brother in prison was, or how much money he possessed: questions that to us would seem the height of vulgarity, to him are simple and natural. Perhaps it is because of his extreme simplicity that his values are reversed.'

'Oh Uncle, how long-winded you are,' said Diana, smiling. Her uncle smiled himself and rose from his chair.

'I still think it would be unwise to ask too many questions,' he replied. 'However, I think I'll take a walk before dinner.' He strolled from the veranda, vanished through the stockade.

'Your uncle's right,' said Jack. 'It isn't very wise to ask strange questions in a strange country. He should know after being here thirty years. Good Lord — thirty years! Whatever does he do for amusement?'

'He's quite happy,' Diana answered. 'At heart I think he enjoys living as simple a life as the people he tries to convert. He often goes for long walks — he's away for hours at a time. He isn't afraid of anything round here, and the people love him. He's always helping them in some way, and I think they realize that inside he's more of a spiritual brother of theirs than he is a Westerner. I mean in liking the little things, and being content to lead a life as near to nature as possible.'

'But how about yourself? Don't you ever get lonely for something more than this?'

A shadow crossed the girl's face. She nodded acquiescence. 'I do — very often. Although Uncle is quite nice, and has taken good care of me, I sometimes feel that he'd rather I wasn't around. He loves being alone.'

They talked a while longer until the Reverend Harper returned, and went in to dinner in a pleasant mood. The missionary seemed to have forgotten his forebodings of the afternoon, and talked wittily and learnedly of various aspects of Chinese life and religion. Dinner over, they all retired to the veranda again.

Conversation languished, and by and by, from the direction of the reverend's chair, issued a prodigious snore, followed by a loud whistling grunt.

'Holy smoke!' exclaimed the American, jumping. 'What's that?'

'Just Uncle snoring,' said Diana with a smile. 'He always makes an awful noise when he takes his after-dinner nap out here.'

'Hmm! Say, Miss Harper — '

'Let's not be conventional,' said the girl softly. 'There isn't any need for you to call me Miss Harper — Diana will do. And I'll call you Jack.'

'That's fine. Diana, then — do you really think that the local boys might know something about the Purple Dragon?'

'I don't know for certain, but I think they may give you some sort of clue. Surprising what retentive memories they have.'

'I'd sure like to speak to one of them about it,' said Jack thoughtfully.

'Why, if you want to it's simple. Suppose we walk along to Layosan's — you remember the little man whose home I damaged with my bike? He's a friend of mine, and has lived all his life in these parts. He may be able to give you a hint.'

'That'd be swell. But how about your uncle?'

'Oh, we'll leave him there. He won't wake up for ages, and even if he did he wouldn't care to come along with us, I'm sure.'

They left the mission station silently

and walked out into the mimosa-scented night. Jack took Diana's arm and noticed she was shivering a little, since it was a cold night. There was a clear, pale moon riding the sky, but as they neared the town the squalid frail homes of the people began to cast deep shadows over the narrow streets.

The river glistened smoothly, reflecting the moonbeams in a kind of glow above it, and a small sampan drifted aimlessly down river. From beneath the doorway of Layosan's home penetrated a thin crack of light from a lantern. Diana tapped, and the door opened to admit her and her companion.

Squatting about the room cross-legged, eating their evening meal from bowls, were four small children and Layosan. As he saw who was visiting him, he sprang to his feet, bowed low, and said: 'I am honoured that you should visit my so-humble home, little white sister. Pray to excuse this unworthy family of mine, which I will send from us.' He turned to his wife and children and instructed them to complete the meal in the inner room. They vanished from sight, the smallest child directing injured glances at the intruders.

'And now that that unworthy rabble has departed,' said Layosan, smiling, 'what can I do for little white sister?'

'My friend, the man-without-a-memory — please call him Jack — wishes to ask you a question, Layosan.'

'I have heard of the case of the white man,' said Layosan, nodding, 'and I am honoured by his presence in my miserable abode. If I can aid him in any way, that I will do.'

'Many thanks, Layosan,' said Jack with a smile. 'During the time of my great sleep, often there crossed my mind a phrase which it seemed should mean much to me. It was of this phrase that I wished to ask you — if you can tell me what or where the Purple Dragon is, and what the name implies?'

Layosan's reaction was instantaneous and alarming. He recoiled a step and, although the bland inscrutability of his countenance remained unchanged, the watchers could detect his nervousness in the twitching of his yellow fingers.

'The Purple Dragon?' he breathed in almost a whisper. Jack nodded eagerly. The Chinaman recovered himself, and his slanted eyes peered at Jack. He said, 'I have heard of it — much. Before the honourable war with our enemies, it was a great Tong which flourished in Liang-Sin. Many people were killed, and it was believed that a certain number of men led it. However, the authorities of our gracious Emperor stepped in and broke up the Tong, putting to death those who were caught. All the lesser members were executed — but not one of the leaders could be traced or named.'

'But you are certain that the Tong was finished before the war with Japan?'

Layosan lowered his voice still further, and said, 'No, I am not certain. It is said now that those same leaders direct the operations of the pirates and outlaws who infest the hills. It is said that such was their rage against the magnificent govern-ment, that they did all they could to put obstacles in the way of progress. It is even said that the heads of the Tong meet here, in Liang-Sin, still. But men close their ears to all these sayings, for it is well known that only death awaits the curious.'

'Layosan,' said Diana, 'it is important for Jack to find out all he can concerning the Purple Dragon. Perhaps you will tell us where the Tong leaders were supposed to meet?'

'Little white sister,' replied Layosan, 'because of what you have done for me in the days that are gone, I will show you and Jack where the Tong used to meet. And now,' he continued philosophically, 'there can be no danger! For was not the street in which rumour had it they assembled, blown up in the great earthquake-from-the-skies?'

'You mean the street was — destroyed in a bombing raid?' said Jack excitedly. Layosan nodded gravely. 'It looks as if we might have something!' exclaimed Jack with enthusiasm. 'I was hit in a raid, and all I remember are the words 'the Purple Dragon'. Now it seems that their headquarters was destroyed — possibly in the same raid!'

Layosan prepared calmly to show them the spot which rumour had it was the base — or had been the base — of the Tong. Within ten minutes they were slipping through streets garishly lit with hanging lanterns, past rows of single-storey dwellings, threading their way through the heart of Liang-Sin, into the old quarter.

Finally they arrived at a section which was in pitch darkness, except for the ineffectual rays of the moon. So dark was the quarter they had reached that even the moonbeams seemed unable to penetrate its gloomy streets and gaunt, half-wrecked structures.

'This is the portion of the town which was completely wiped out in the great earthquake-from-above,' Layosan informed them very quietly. 'It is a dead patch, without life or light. Walk carefully, little white sister, for there is much wreckage here.'

With the aid of the light from Diana's flashlight, they traced their way through the lifeless streets. There was something unwholesome and eerie about the place, as if ghouls and spectres, killed by unendurable violence, haunted the narrow paths, lurked unseen behind the ragged outlines of crumbling buildings, and peered with lascivious eyes from the blank holes in the walls which had once represented windows.

Shortly they came to a street more badly battered than the rest. 'It is down here — what is left,' Layosan informed them. 'It was almost completely destroyed. They found no bodies in the rubble and wreckage.'

'Can you find it?' enquired Jack.

'I think that I can,' Layosan told him. 'Please to follow!'

'Don't move!' said Diana suddenly. She switched off her light hastily. 'I've got a feeling we're being shadowed — I thought I could hear footsteps.'

Frozen into immobility, the three stood silently, listening. There was no sound audible, save the sighing of a gentle breeze which was sweeping in from the river. Then:

*Thwok!*

It was a weird, soft sound, and for a second neither Diana nor Jack could place it. And then Layosan, who had been silhouetted against a tumbled-down wall, gave a short, coughing gasp, and crumpling at the knees, fell before them.

Diana screamed and Jack, jumping swiftly from the shadow of the wall which concealed them, lifted the Chinaman into safety. Rapidly he bent above Layosan and noticed the short ornamental hatchet which was buried in the back of the man's skull, buried deep.

'He's — dead,' he whispered, and gazed silently at Diana's white face, visible as a blur in the gloom.

'The — the hatchet man!' breathed Diana, panic clutching at nerves. Jack nodded without speaking. Diana shuddered again. She said, 'A lot of the Tongs have a man to perform executions — it's generally decided by drawing lots.'

'Listen,' whispered Jack, 'we have to get away from here! I think they're hiding somewhere, waiting for us to show ourselves. The moment we make good targets, they'll start throwing. We can't do anything for Layosan, so we may as well try to escape ourselves.'

'But — but how?'

Jack reflected a moment. Then he

indicated the wall on the right. He hissed, 'If we can slide over that we may be able to dodge them. It's a low wall, and overshadowed by the one next to it — I don't think they'll spot us unless we make a racket. Will you go first?'

Diana knew it was no time to argue, and although her knees were hammering violently against one another, she agreed. With Jack close behind her she edged towards the deepest patch of shadow. Cautiously she rose, reached for the top of the rotting woodwork and, helped by Jack, slid up and over the other side.

She was hardly down when Jack, glancing round, became aware of darker shadows just along the street — shadows moving towards him! Soft shuffling noises were audible; then all subterfuge was thrown to the wind, and the shadows took definite shape and commenced racing along the street towards him.

He vaulted lightly up to the top of the woodwork and felt the wind of the hatchet which hissed past his head. Then he was down the other side and, grabbing Diana by the arm, had started to run.

As they raced through the dark, deserted streets piled high with the debris from the raid, he experienced a queer sensation that this had happened to him before. Not only happened before, but in these very streets. It was all so familiar: the swift patter of pursuing footsteps, the harsh clatter of his own European shod feet along the street. But then he hadn't had anyone with him; there hadn't been a girl along, and something had happened! What? An air raid — that was the answer! And then the nearness of the pursuers caused him to drive other things from his mind; to concentrate only on putting as much space between them as possible.

Abruptly the semi-demolished buildings ended, and they were dashing wildly over a patch of loamy soil. Ahead of them was a rice field, stretching out monotonously under the cold, clear moonlight.

Still clutching Diana tightly, he dashed on, into the sloppy ground of the rice patch. Ten yards in he threw himself flat, dragging Diana with him. The intensely irrigated soil squelched over their bodies, concealing them. Carefully he raised his head so that he could see over the damp, squat walls of earth which surrounded the field.

The pursuers had broken into the open and were standing at the edge of the patch, staring keenly in every direction. There was a tall, brutal-looking Chinese, naked except for a loin-cloth; his face was an expressionless mask of blubber, hideous in the wan glow from the moon. He was minus one eye. With him were two more slightly smaller Chinamen. Once more something clicked in Jack's brain; once more he found his memory beginning to function. He was certain beyond doubt that he knew these men, particularly the giant — Chala! The name came to him in a flash. But where and when had he met him? And in what circumstances?

'They must have broken off in the ruins — they have tricked us!' snarled one of the smaller men. 'Let us return and search there!'

The three of them turned and retreated into the ruins. Jack watched them go and then rose to his knees. With Diana at his side, muddy and miserable, they began to crawl through the rice field. The area was greater than they had assumed; and once, when a portion of over-irrigated ground sloped abruptly away, Diana went completely under. She came up coated with nauseous, clammy mud, a most peculiar odour emanating from her.

Hours later, it seemed, they arrived wet and worn at the mission station. The Reverend Harper eyed them both with considerable surprise and a little suspicion, but on being informed of the facts he undertook to see about reporting the murder of poor Layosan to the appropriate authorities.

The bedraggled couple each took a bath from a tin affair which the mission sported, and after a hot drink sat for a while discussing the affair.

'There's one thing,' stated Jack, grimly. 'Previously, all I wanted to find this Purple Dragon gang for was to find out who I am — if they know. But now, after what happened to that poor devil Layosan, I want them for something more personal. And believe me, I'll get them!'

Meanwhile, in another quarter of the town, a languid Westernized young Chinese lady received and committed to memory certain instructions delivered to her by letter. After which, the letter and its contents were committed to the fire.

# 6

## Mark of the Purple Dragon

Jack Green yawned prodigiously, slipped off the embroidered Chinese robe which Diana had lent to him while his own things were cleaned and dried, and prepared to slide between the sheets.

There were two pillows on the bed, and Jack had found while at the hospital that he slept much better on a low pillow. Therefore he pulled the top one away and carried it over to a cane chair out of the way. Then, in the feeble rays from the lamp, he caught sight of something which brought him up with a start. Stooping, he examined the pillow and extracted from it a thin needle of bamboo, the end of which bore a grim brown stain. It had been protruding exactly from the centre of the pillow, so placed that had he lain his head upon it, it would have pierced the skin.

His jaw set grimly as he wrapped it in a handkerchief and stowed it away. He didn't need two guesses to know that it was a poisoned shoot — possibly placed in his pillow while he and Diana had been out and the reverend sleeping. But it pointed to one thing: that to know which room he was going to occupy, the Tong must have spies in the mission station itself!

His thoughts ran briefly over the servants: Ching, a young native, a kind of general factotum; Zuki, the very, very old gardener; and Tayo, the Chinese houseboy. Anyone of them could have slipped the needle into the pillow.

Before he climbed between the sheets, he carefully examined every inch of the bed. There was nothing more which might have injured or killed him.

Jack lay back and tried again to flog his faulty memory into action. Things were becoming clearer now — he was convinced that he had seen Chala before, and that he had been running from someone when the bomb had fallen. But beyond that, try as he might, there was only a blank nothingness save for the sinister words 'the Purple Dragon'.

Quite obviously the secret Tong wished to kill him. But why? Had he in his past done the gang some disservice? Or did he know something about them, something which they were afraid he would reveal? This seemed the most likely theory, and musing on it, Jack fell into a troubled sleep.

He was awakened by Ching, who entered bearing a cup of tea. His clothing had been cleaned spotlessly while he had slept, and was now laid out ready for him. He washed and dressed hurriedly.

The reverend and his niece were already at breakfast when he emerged from his room. They greeted him with smiles, and the missionary told him that he had reported the matter of Layosan's death, and that there would be some questions to answer down in the town after breakfast.

Jack and Diana went down alone, since the reverend stated that he had some work to do. The powers-that-be were perfunctory in their questions; seemingly they were not greatly affected by the death of Layosan, and were intolerant of being put to any trouble to record the details of the murder. But Jack learned that the body of the dead man, when brought in, had had a crude paper dragon, coloured purple, attached with a pin to the abdomen.

After the questioning they walked around the town for a time, finding it very much different to the place of death and horror it had been the previous night. Wandering aimlessly, they came to the part where the bomb damage commenced.

It looked innocent and harmless enough in the broad daylight, but Diana could not repress a shudder as she gazed down it. Jack, however, was eager to locate the point at which they had had to give up their attempt to find the old headquarters of the Tong the night before, and from there to carry on.

It seemed absurd to express any fear in the daylight, so Diana agreed to go with him. They found the point at which Layosan had been murdered without any difficulty, and then they traced a path down the street he had indicated to them as having housed the base of the Purple Dragon Tong.

Here, halfway down the street, they found that which they sought. The place had been badly battered, and the walls from the building above had all but blocked up the cellar beneath; but on the visible portions of the cellar walls could be distinguished the top half of a painted dragon. More vague memories stirred in Jack's mind, but his brain still refused to focus.

On the return journey to the mission station, Jack told Diana of the poisoned bamboo shoot he had discovered in his bed. She was horrified, and insisted that the servants should be questioned immediately; but the American persuaded her that they would not only learn nothing by that, but that they would put the would-be murderer on his guard. In the end she agreed that it would be best to say nothing, but rather to keep both ears and eyes open for any suspicious behaviour on the part of the servants.

They decided that it would not do to mention the matter even to the reverend, since he would probably be furious about it and take it on himself to haul the servants over the coals.

They spent a very pleasant afternoon, Diana telling him of the terrors of the floods which had occurred two years ago when the dammed-up Hoang Ho had burst its banks and flooded hundreds of miles of the surrounding country. After dinner the reverend suggested that Jack might like to take a walk into the town with him, to a small tea shop he knew of, where excellent brandy could be obtained at a price. Jack was by no means averse and, leaving Diana to read some of the latest magazines from America and England, they set off for the town.

'Funny thing,' mused the reverend as they walked along, 'but this little place I'm taking you to is where most Europeans who come to Liang-Sin finally find their way.'

'What's funny about that, sir?' questioned Jack. 'If they sell good brandy, it's only natural.'

'Yes, yes, m'boy, I grant you that! But the funny thing is how they ever find it! It's tucked away in one of the most dismal little streets imaginable, you know, and from the outside it looks like nothing on earth. But you shall see for yourself shortly.'

It was exactly as the reverend had said. The Café of the Lotus Leaf was dirty and decrepit beyond words on the outside, but within a startling transformation was wrought. Colourful lanterns hung from chains of imitation lotus flowers near the ceiling. Rustling bamboo curtains shielded each little alcove from its neighbour, and the chairs were strewn with costly silken cushions. Over in one corner a small orchestra played the weird and flutelike music of the East; and scattered about the place were men and women of many nationalities.

The reverend — who, although a missionary, was obviously not a teetotaler — ordered drinks which were served in long-stemmed glasses. While they drank, Jack glanced through the curtain which half-concealed them. The place was filling up, and Chinese girls were hurrying to and fro attending to the needs of the customers.

After the second round the reverend looked at his watch; he then emitted an annoyed exclamation and said, 'I'm dashed sorry, m'boy, but I have a call to make while I'm here in the town. Perhaps you wouldn't mind waiting here for me? I'll only be about twenty minutes.'

'By all means,' replied Jack courteously. 'This place fascinates me — I've no objection to waiting at all.'

'Fine, fine! Well, I must rush!'

The reverend, going at a good rate of knots, vanished into the outer world again. Jack relaxed in his chair and prepared for an interesting wait.

Idly he began to muse on the probable nationalities of the various patrons he could see from behind the bamboo screen. Over on the left was a Russian — obviously a Russian, with a great black beard and deep-sunken dark eyes. A few tables from him, almost concealed by the folds of a bead curtain, sat a man and a young girl; Jack could not place the

62

nationality of the man, but the girl, he thought at a guess, was probably a Mongolian type.

Then his roving eyes suddenly became riveted on a woman he had not previously noticed. She was seated in the cubicle almost directly opposite, and had the appearance of a half-caste girl born of Chinese and Western parentage. Her high cheekbones lent a haughty, superior look to her beautifully modulated features, and her slanted almond eyes bore a look of mystery and invitation. She was leaning forward, elbows resting lightly on the table, black-gloved fingers toying idly with the stem of her wine glass. Her position served to emphasize the graceful, sweeping lines of her figure, as did her knee-length black dress, clinging tightly to every curve and angle.

But the thing which most riveted Jack's attention was her smile — for it was directed, unashamedly, straight at him. Whatever he had been in the past, Jack was aware of one thing: women intrigued him deeply. And as he caught her glance, he raised his glass gallantly and drained it of the liquor. The woman's smile widened and her eyes half-closed sleepily. Jack could imagine her purring like a cat.

She beckoned to one of the waitresses, scribbled a few lines on a scrap of paper and indicated Jack. The waitress smiled and brought the paper over. The message was short, but concise: 'Forgive me for staring so rudely, but I think that I have seen you somewhere before. Could it have been in America?'

Jack crumpled the paper up and stowed it in his pocket. He rose, crossed the floor, and sank into the chair next to her. She gave him a welcoming smile.

'You must think I'm awfully — how do you say? — fresh, Mr . . . ?' she said in a deep, throbbing voice.

Jack waved his hand airily. 'Of course not, Miss . . . ?'

'My name is Lili.' She smiled. 'Lili Lee.'

'Thank you, Lili,' said Jack coolly. 'My name — I think — is Green, Jack Green. At least, that's the name I'm known by at present.'

'You talk in riddles, Mr. Green. You

*think?* That is the name you are known by *at present?* I do not understand.'

'No more than do I,' Jack told her, smiling. 'I'm afraid I lost my memory some months ago. In fact, with you stating in your note that you thought you had seen me in America, I wondered if you could throw any light on my real identity.'

The Oriental girl pursed her lips in perplexity. She said, 'I'm — I'm afraid not, Mr. Green. You see, I feel sure I have seen you somewhere back in America — but I can't recall any of the circumstances connected with the meeting. It may not even have been a meeting — just a casual glance, perhaps.'

'It doesn't really matter,' Jack told her. 'I suppose I can't expect you to recall a name just by a face. So you have been to America?'

She smiled a little and said, 'I hope so. I was born there. My father was Chinese, my mother an American woman.' She said it quite frankly, as if she thought that nobody would attach shame to such a liaison. Jack found himself liking her and her frankness more than ever. The exotic perfume which she wore filled the tiny cubicle, enchanting him. Her dark eyes rested on his own, pools of enticing excitement. Her very presence, the way she moved her sleek body, filled him with voluptuous desires. There was something about her — something magnetic, intoxicating his mind and limbs; something which Western girls, with their shallow beauty, had not. Something which even Diana Harper could not lay claim to, for all her English sweetness.

And yet, Jack knew it was a dangerous quality. The smile was not a friendly smile: it was a smile which hinted at the gratification of dark and secret desires — a wild hour of turgid passion — but to Jack it seemed it was not meant for him alone, but for all men; any men. And underneath it was that undertone — that certain cold, cruel quality; an iciness beneath those liquid pools of wantonness; beneath those moist, full lips. A quality which, inanely, made Jack think of the black widow spider which ate her mate after the nuptials.

'Of what are you thinking?' came the woman's soft voice.

Jack pulled himself together with a start, realizing he had neither said nor done anything for the last three minutes, while he had been held by the near-hypnotic strangeness of her gaze.

He smiled and said, 'My thoughts really aren't worth a thing.'

'Really? I'm sure they must be. A man like you — so much mystery about you, it seems — must think strange things.'

'If you insist upon knowing, my thoughts were about you,' he told her.

'Oh, but now you must tell me what you thought!'

'If I did, I assure you you would slap my face!' He grinned.

'Would I?' she said softly; and looking into those eyes again, and through them into her very soul, he knew she wouldn't.

'My father,' she said, unexpectedly picking up her remarks at the point she had left off minutes before, 'owned a chain of laundries. Very profitable. He and my mother died five years ago, and I found myself a very rich woman. For a long time — all through the war — I amused myself with the attractions which America had to offer. But all the time I felt a strange, deep wish to see my ancestors' native land. China! The East! They called to me with a call which could not be denied. And so,' she went on, 'when the war ended I came here as soon as possible. I hired a sampan large enough to accommodate myself and one servant. I began to travel up the Hoang Ho.

'I was enthralled. I touched at all the major cities along the river, spent a day at each. Finally I reached Liang-Sin, and here I am.' She finished speaking, twisting her glass stem round rapidly.

'There is only one thing,' she went on, returning Jack's gaze squarely. 'It is a very lonely life. I fear that Chinese men have no appeal for me. I must confess my love life ended when I left America.'

'I think I understand,' Jack said slowly.

'Do you?' Her voice was low, seductive. Her eyes fastened onto his, smouldering with suppressed desire. 'Do you?' she repeated.

Jack tried to escape from the spell of

those eyes; tried to bring himself back to sanity. It was too melodramatic to have any vestige of reality, he was sure. And yet — that perfume, those eyes, the allure of the curved body . . .

'I'm sure I do,' he replied earnestly. 'Loneliness can be a damning thing — I know it only too well! How do you think I felt that month at the hospital? A man without identity, without name or relations — a man without anyone in the wide world who'd give a damn what happened to him. It's a lousy feeling.'

Lili Lee's eyes were now veiled almost entirely by her long, dark lashes. Suddenly they opened, resting on his strong, manly features; his dark, wavy hair. She said meaningfully, 'A man such as yourself need never be lonely — Jack.'

Jack felt the blood flushing to his cheeks; his mouth felt suddenly dry and hard. He said, 'You mean . . . ?'

She nodded. Her gloved hand moved across the table and found his. Her touch was electric, sending a tremor the length of his spine. 'I mean — exactly that which you desire me to mean,' she said softly.

'Or, if that is too straightforward for you, perhaps you would care to return to my houseboat with me tonight. I have there many photographs of America, and if you were to look through them, who knows? It may restore some vestige of memory to you. If you are an American, there are sure to be many things you must have seen in your past — the Empire State Building, the Statue of Liberty, Madison Square Garden. I mention only a few of the more important. Surely among such a collection as I have, you will know and remember some of the scenes.'

Jack knew that the photographs were introduced merely as an added inducement — or as a gesture to the proprieties which forbid such visits as Lili Lee suggested. But even without mention of the photographs he would have accompanied her — he could not have resisted! He was finding out that where women were concerned, his past character must have been lamentably weak — and still was.

Lili Lee became impatient at his momentary silence. 'Of course,' she said, 'if your morals argue against a man and woman alone — save for one servant — in a houseboat on a river late in the evening, it is unfortunate. I hadn't thought that you might be one of those strong, silent American adventurers who thrust from them with an iron will any such improper situations.'

'I'm not,' admitted Jack. 'Those guys only exist in novels — I guess I haven't ever met up with anyone like that in my life. It isn't that I don't relish your proposal, but that I am supposed to be waiting here for an acquaintance of mine.'

'Could you not leave a note for him?'

'Of course! That would be the simplest solution . . . '

She handed him a pen and a piece of paper. Hastily he scribbled a few lines to the reverend. 'Tell him,' she said, 'that you are on the track of your lost identity — tell him that you may be away a few days.'

'*A few days?*' echoed Jack.

'But of course,' she replied, giving him a languorous look. 'Surely you would not be so ungentlemanly as to break up a beautiful friendship which shows so much

71

— promise? And if you fail to mention the length of time which you may be away, it is possible your friend will think you have suffered a renewed attack of amnesia, and be worried accordingly.'

Jack found it hard to accept the fact that this woman was suggesting to a man who had been a stranger fifteen minutes earlier, what she obviously was suggesting. It seemed the woman read his thoughts, for she smiled and said: 'You find my ways — strange? But they are not — not really. All my life I have had all I wanted until now. Now I want more than anything the company of an American man. After all, what is convention? Write as I directed, please, Jack.'

Almost stunned by the unreality of it, Jack did as he was asked. Lili folded the note and handed it to a waitress. Jack gave her instructions as to whom it should be given. And then they left the Lotus Leaf.

She led him through the rapidly darkening streets, by a route he had not traversed hitherto, to the dammed-up banks of the river. Here, some way out of the town, the dim form of a Chinese sampan loomed up, moored to the bank.

It was a compact, freshly painted boat, as Jack could see before they had even boarded it. It lay motionless on the placid surface of the treacherous waters — those same waters which carried so much silt that at times they dammed their own course, and the flood burst through the high banks, bringing disaster and misery to those who lived along their borders.

But at present the river was calm and serene, mirroring the face of the pallid moon in its black depths; the flat-bottomed house boat floated solidly on the surface, like a black hole in the moon-tinted waters.

They clambered aboard; Lili led the way to the squat cabin which dominated almost the entire area of the deck. 'I had this boat specially built,' she explained. 'The cabin is divided into three compartments — one which I use as kitchen and dining room, one as my own bedroom, and the third where my little servant girl sleeps. Two extremely brawny gentlemen sail and pole the boat for me, but they spend the nights on land since there is no room here for them. I hope you are not hungry? Chee Cho, my servant girl, does all the cooking for me, and she will be asleep now, I fear.'

'I am hungry only for you,' Jack told her. She smiled her sultry smile again, slid one black-clad arm about his neck, and in the deep shadows of the cabin drew his face down, until her red lips pressed tightly against his own. At the touch of those sensuous lips, Jack would have crushed her to him there and then; but she suddenly moved lightly away, gazing back at him tantalizingly from the open doorway of the cabin.

Controlling his emotions, Jack stepped inside and felt her smooth hand, now ungloved, catch his own. 'Come,' she whispered, guiding him through the darkness of the room. 'We will go to the bedroom, where it is more comfortable. There I have various cocktails which I brought with me from New York. I could not bear to deny myself the luxuries of a good 'old-fashioned'!' she concluded with a ripple of laughter.

They went through a second door, then Lili busied herself lighting three lamps. Their rays penetrated only dimly through the orange shades, but nevertheless Jack was enabled to see that the sleeping compartment was furnished in Western style with the exception of a number of rugs of Eastern design.

'Please make yourself comfortable,' Lili told him. 'I must slip into something more appropriate.' She vanished behind an ornate screen in the corner, and Jack heard the rustle of silk as she changed her attire. He sat on a low divan, waiting impatiently for her reappearance, his senses keyed up to the limit.

Shortly she came from behind the screen, and Jack's breath caught in his throat as he looked at her. She now wore an almost transparent negligée, and dimly visible beneath were the latest effusions of Parisian design. Softly and alluringly she moved across the room towards him, like some graceful cat — or tigress!

'And now,' she said, 'first of all — a cocktail. Let us drink to our new — friendship!' She crossed to a modern cocktail cabinet and poured drinks from a bottle. She came back with the glasses, her eyes bewitching the young American.

Impulsively he reached up and drew her beside him to the divan.

'Jack!' she exclaimed. 'Please, not so rough! See, you almost spilled the drinks!'

'What kind of woman are you, Lili?' he demanded. 'What damned exotic power do you hold that makes a usually sensible chap like myself go overboard for you?'

She smiled once more and said: 'Don't be so romantic, Jack. Let's look on this whole affair as a matter of convenience rather than romance, shall we? Drink your cocktail.'

He did so, then laid the glass aside impatiently. Once more he reached out for her, and this time she succumbed, sinking softly, with all the roundness of her, into his arms. The fragrance of the perfume on her clothing mingled with the subtle aroma of the white lilies which she threaded into her hair on each side of her head.

Casting whatever control he had left aside, Jack drew his hand gently over her black waves, then turned her head half-sideways so that her face was no more than an inch from his own. Her eyes closed, lips slightly parted in complete surrender. Almost brutally he pressed his lips to hers, and held there.

But unexpectedly Lili tore herself away, jumped to her feet, and retreated to the far side of the room. Jack gazed after her, feeling his head spinning. 'What — what's wrong?' he gasped.

'You fool,' she sneered. 'You Americans think you're such lady-killers, so clever! You thought you were about to add a further conquest to your collection, didn't you? And all the time I was playing with you!'

Jack rose to his feet and tried to move towards her. The dizzy sensation in his head was rapidly getting worse.

'I don't understand . . . '

The girl, her face twisted into a mask of contempt, spat in his direction. She said, 'You will understand, Mr. Green. That cocktail you drank was drugged!'

As if to prove her words, the room began to spin in front of Jack's eyes. Weakly he tried to walk, but his legs refused to function properly. He felt himself toppling, falling; then his head struck the floor, and before he lost consciousness he was aware of Lili Lee's evil laughter . . .

# 7

## The Temple with Seven Walls

How long he was in the grip of that drugged slumber Jack could not have said. He was beset by dreams — horrific nightmares in which he found himself plodding knee-deep in slime through miasmic swamps which were old when civilization was still young; pursued and threatened by monstrous winged dragons, their ugly, razor-sharp talons dripping with purple gore; wandering aimlessly but fearfully through gloomy prehistoric forests where lived a race of monoculous cyclops. And always behind it all, behind every thick-boled tree, came that obscene laughter: the laughter of an evil woman; a woman who would make love to men to lead them to their disaster. And again, behind the laughter, looking wraith-like through that misty world in which his mind wandered, were the eyes of Lili Lee

— those dark, hypnotic, treacherous eyes.

From time to time his drug-crazed consciousness would struggle halfway back to reality: he would feel the motion of the sampan as it drifted slowly down the river; and then he would sink back into that nightmare world from which he had emerged, gripped by a horror that he was no more, and that this was death!

Now and then, during his abysmal roamings, he would feel his face being moved; would feel food and liquid pushed into his mouth and would, almost subconsciously, masticate it. And there would be a voice, one he knew, which would say, 'How do you feel, Mr. Green? Mr. Green? Still out!'

Mr. Green, Mr. Green, Mr. Green; the words would revolve endlessly in his mind while he journeyed in the fantastic limbo of the netherworld; then it would become confused and vague until the words faded, and he was enveloped in stygian gloom.

For what seemed eternity he roamed, until above him there shone a pale light, far off in the blackness, flickering feebly.

He struggled upwards towards it, praying that he might reach it and escape from the eternal dimness; and gradually it drew nearer, as with all his soul he fought his way back to life again.

The light was that of a lamp suspended from the ceiling of the cramped, odiferous cubicle in which he was a prisoner. As full awareness penetrated to him, he found that he could not move either hands or legs, both being securely roped, and the ropes passed under the truckle bed on which he lay.

Through a crack in the coarse wooden walls he could see that it was daylight, but whether he had lain here for hours or for days — or even months — he could not tell. He judged that he was still on Lili Lee's sampan, and that this was the room she claimed was given over to her servant. But it was apparent that the room had not been lived in for years — therefore, Lili Lee had been lying about her maid. And if she had lied on one score she had most likely lied on them all.

He cursed himself futilely as he thought what a fool he had been. Deceived by the lure of an Eastern siren, he had thrown away his freedom, probably his life! He swore savagely to himself that if ever he escaped from the mess he was in, he would never believe another woman!

There was a fumbling at the door; it opened, and outlined in the rays of the sun, Lili Lee stood there smiling. She looked every inch Chinese now, wearing a figured tea-gown and a link of jade stones round her neck. Jack reflected that he would have liked to get that neck between his fingers and squeeze the breath from her body . . .

'Good afternoon, my amorous one,' she said, speaking in the Chinese language. 'I trust that the drug-of-sweet-dreams was not too strong for your palate?'

'Exactly what is your set-up?' demanded Jack harshly.

She sneered. '*That* you shall see for yourself, Mr. Green. What fools you Westerners are! You haven't an ounce of artifice or cunning in your entire bodies. We of the East always look under the mask which we see. We ourselves wear a mask continually — perhaps that is why we are so suspicious. But you white fools carry your hearts — and hopes — on your sleeves! If you feel desire you permit it to shine from your face like a beacon — little thinking that it might prove a weapon in the hands of your enemies. If you feel hate, you show that also, thus putting the hated one on his guard. If you feel love, you are, towards the one you adore, affectionate, tender, possessive: you do not know love as we here in the East know it. You have no conception of the delights there are in tormenting, hurting, someone you hold more dear to you than life itself!'

'Did you bring me here to treat me to a discourse on your damnable sadistic philosophy?' grated Jack. She flushed angrily. Jack went on: 'I know all about it. You hold life cheap out here in the East! Other people's lives! But if it came to your own there's one hell of a squawk! Don't talk to me about wearing the mask — I'm damned if I'd care to wear the mask people like you adopt. You're living a lie half the time. No wonder your race progresses slowly!

'That's enough,' snapped Lili Lee. 'You Westerners wouldn't understand our ways. You can never hope to — our ways are as alien as a saxophone playing in a symphony orchestra.'

'I can well believe that. And now, suppose you tell me where in hell you're taking me?'

'You know,' said the girl, 'It has just occurred to me that you have changed in some strange way since you have been under the drug. Your conversation, I mean. It's so much more colourful now — could it be that you are regaining your old personality? I must confess I like you much better in this mood.'

'You'll permit me the liberty of not giving a damn what you like or dislike, I hope?' said the American ironically.

'You aren't very tractable, are you, Mr. Green? But then you have a good reason for feeling annoyed, I admit. You asked me where in hell I was taking you. Well, I have no objection to answering that question. We are journeying down to a point midway between Weinan and Tungkwan — a matter of about a hundred miles from Liang-Sin. There we will take to the land and travel some thirty miles further towards the hills of Kwang-Wo. Here, nestling in the foot of these hills, is the Temple of the Purple Dragon — a most magnificent structure with seven walls. There is a rather interesting story about those walls, Mr. Green. Would you care to hear it?'

'Don't bother, Miss Lee.'

'No bother, Mr. Green,' she said, ignoring the sarcasm. 'Long ago, when Confucius was teaching, this temple was built by his followers. It was here, from time to time, that he came to escape the harshness of the outside world and to continue his writings. Long after his death Confucians worshipped at this shrine, but it was so badly placed and so inaccessible that after a number of years it fell into disuse. Nor was it used again until hundreds of years had passed. And then the great war lord, Ko Ken, being mortally afraid of the enemies he had made on his pillaging and territorial raids, decided it would be the ideal spot for him to end his days in peace.

'But there was no peace for such a cruel and unjust man as Ko Ken had been! Assassinations were continually attempted, and were foiled, but each attempt caused Ko Ken great uneasiness. So, after each attempt had failed, he built a fresh wall about the place to make assurance doubly sure.

'For seven men who tried to murder Ko Ken, there sprang up seven walls, the bodies of the would-be assassins being buried under their particular edifice. But even seven walls were not enough, Mr. Green. For one dark night, Ko Ken was found lying dead in his chamber, his head cleft from scalp to chin — by one of his own servants!'

'A suitable end,' sneered Jack. 'And where, exactly, does the Purple Dragon fit in?'

'The temple has been the headquarters of the Tong for the last twenty-five years, Mr. Green. The Purple Dragon Tong was a religious cult which flourished long ago — but eventually it stood in danger of dying out. It was then that a certain gentleman, who already controlled the activities of large bands of Chinese outlaws and pirates, conceived the idea of taking over the name. It was a good idea, for the Tong was held in great awe by the simple natives, who had heard weird stories of blood sacrifices and such things. It was successful as a blind to prevent people enquiring too closely into the activities of its members.

'In this way the gentleman, who had been joined by certain eminent townsmen of Liang-Sin, was able to amass a considerable fortune. But alas, the government heard of these activities, and stepping in they successfully broke up the bands of pirates and outlaws who comprised the lesser members of the organization.

'Naturally, the leaders had to find some new headquarters to operate from — somewhere obscure, away from Liang-Sin — and the old Confucian temple seemed ideal, as it has proved to be. Once they were firmly established, the leaders began to organize their gangs again, and all the loot was taken to the temple and stored there.'

'And that's where you're taking me?'

'Precisely.'

'But I can't understand why the Tong

should want me. What have I ever done in my past that should make them so relentless? You must know, if you are a member of the Tong — you must know who I am, what I have done, everything! It can hardly matter now, since I probably won't get away alive, so why not set my mind at rest by telling me a thing or two?'

For a time the girl was silent. Then she said, 'I am not at liberty to tell you very much, Mr. Green, but I see no harm in telling you your real name, which is Alan Carrol. More I cannot tell you.'

Jack tried vainly to dig up some memories of the name Alan Carrol, but failed. However, since it appeared his name was really this, there could be no sense in continuing to think of himself as Jack Green.

'What was I?' he demanded curiously. 'I mean, how did I come to get mixed up in all this?'

'I can tell you no more,' she said with a shrug. 'Be content that you now know your real name, Mr. — Carrol. And now I will bring you some food. Before long our journey will be ended, and then there is another long journey in front of us, so you must make a good meal now. I have no wish to see you starve, Mr. Carrol.'

She closed the door, and Alan Carrol, as he was now, fidgeted uncomfortably and for the hundredth time tested the strength of the bonds which held him. But they were quite strong, and any hopes he had had of breaking them had to be dismissed as impossible.

Not long after this he became aware of heavy footsteps on the deck. They were approaching his door, and were not the soft cat-like steps of Lili Lee. They paused outside, and Alan remembered what the girl had told him about having two strong men to manoeuvre the sampan for her. He twisted his eyes towards the door, which was slowly opening.

A massive hand entered, bearing a bowl of food. It was followed by a tremendous head, then the rest of the body.

Alan found himself looking at the one-eyed giant, the cyclops who had pursued him through his nightmares and who had been at the edge of the rice field the night Layosan had been killed!

# 8

## The Girl Who Knew Too Much

'Uncle,' said Diana for the twentieth time, 'what on earth can have become of Jack?'

Her uncle, puffing absently at his briar pipe, shook his head wearily. 'I've told you, my dear — when I returned to the Café of the Lotus Leaf he had gone. He left a note saying he had met someone who might be able to help him trace his identity, and he would probably be away a few days. That's all I know.'

'May I see the note?'

The reverend fumbled impatiently in his pocket and unearthed a worn scrap of paper. Diana took it from him, straightened it out and read: 'Forgive me for slipping away like this, sir, but I have bumped into someone who may possibly help me find out who and what I am. If I am away a few days, do not be alarmed. Yours, Jack Green.'

It was simple enough, clear enough. Almost too simple, too clear. Diana had a vague feeling of impending catastrophe. She had formed her opinion of the American, and she hardly thought he would be the type to run off unexpectedly on an unknown errand without informing his friends and host of his intentions. She folded up the paper thoughtfully and thrust it into her pocket.

Her uncle tapped out his pipe and stuffed it into his pocket. He said, 'I'm afraid I'll have to leave you all alone, my dear. I've received a message from Peikan; it appears that new young fellow who's taken over the mission station there has got himself into some sort of a mess. It means a long journey inland, but I must go along and help him out, you know. I'll try to get back before the end of the week.'

Diana nodded. She was used to her uncle suddenly galloping off into what he smilingly called 'the interior', on journeys to other mission stations. Naturally, being senior, these posts called for a great deal of his time. He pushed off into the station to pack the small case he invariably carried with him on these occasions, and Diana opened a parcel which had arrived that day.

Idly she began to unpack the articles it contained. A pair of ear muffs, three pairs of gloves, two cardigans with a quantity of holes in them, a selection of used ties and collars, a pair of worn trousers, and a choice assortment of moths! A note which was enclosed ran: 'From the Maiden Ladies' Society of Biddlecombe-in-the-Wold, for the poor, dear Chinese peasants'.

Diana couldn't help smiling at the weird assortment of goods. She wondered if the dear maiden ladies would have believed that the poor, dear Chinese peasants would have died rather than be seen out in any of the peculiar garments they had sent. She also wondered where the maiden ladies had got hold of the trousers!

She came to the conclusion that probably they were no ladies. Absently she stuffed the garments into a drawer, slipped on a light coat and left the station. She walked down into the town past Layosan's home, round to the Café of the Lotus

Leaf. She entered and secured a small table near the door, where she could keep her eyes on the customers. When the waitress came for her order she ordered tea, and said, 'I'm looking for a friend of mine who comes here — an American gentleman. You wouldn't happen to know if he's been here lately?'

'Oh, yes,' stated the girl. 'He was here but last night. I myself had the honour to serve him. He left with a lady.'

A lady! Diana experienced a keen shock; she found it hard to believe her ears. She said, 'A — a lady? Er, what — what kind of lady?'

'A very beautiful lady,' replied the waitress, straining her memory. 'She was, I should think, a half-caste. She was also well dressed, and had much money. She spoke nicely. In English. I heard some of their conversation, and a little I understood . . . about her sampan, and the river, and some photographs. After a time, the American gentlemen left a note with me for his companion, and left with her.'

Dazedly, Diana thanked her and slipped

some coins into her hand. Forgetting the tea, she stood up and made her way out of the café.

For some time she walked aimlessly about the town; then she found her feet dragging her in the direction of the river. She walked along the banks and shortly came across a spot where a boat had been moored. There was the heavy wooden stake which had been driven into the bank to secure the tie-rope. There were footprints: four sets. One set was of massive feet, naked and clearly outlined. Near to these were the marks made by Chinese padded shoes, and a little further along, the marks of European shoes — one man's, one woman's.

Her mind in a whirl, she turned back towards the mission. The sensation of some unknown peril crowded more strongly upon her as the minutes passed, and by the time she had regained the station she was eaten with a terrible anxiety for Jack's safety.

She burst in on her uncle as he was completing packing. She said, 'Uncle, I've been down to the café. They told me Jack left with a woman — a half-caste woman.'

The reverend gave her a surprised glance. 'Dear me,' he said, shocked. 'I had no idea our young fellow was *that* kind of a chap.'

'Oh, *do* try to understand, Uncle! This girl — she may have been a member of the Purple Dragon gang. Suppose she was sent to trap him? As far as I can make out, they went to a sampan which had been moored in the river. It isn't there now — I looked. But his footprints are — and hers — and two sets of native prints.'

'But what are you trying to imply?' asked her uncle.

'Simply that in some manner, the Purple Dragon Tong have got their hands on Jack! I feel sure of it, Uncle.'

'Nonsense, my girl,' said the reverend with some asperity. 'If your young American friend wants to go gadding about with some half-caste woman in a sampan, then he obviously isn't a fit companion for you — and personally, I am glad to have him out of this station. Dear me, if he's a man like that, there's no telling what might have happened!'

'I can't believe that of him,' said Diana steadily. 'If he hasn't returned by sundown I shall go to the town and put everything I know before the authorities. I shall tell them that I think he's met with foul play, and I don't care what they think! I'll insist on an investigation! Now we know he's gone in a sampan, it shouldn't be very hard to trace it and its owner.'

Her uncle shook his head. He said, 'For Heaven's sake, child, don't butt your head into things like this! It may be more dangerous than you imagine. Listen, I'll tell you what: do nothing until I get back. Then, if your friend hasn't returned, I personally will attend to the matter. Do you understand?'

'No, Uncle, I'm sorry! That might be too late. Unless he comes back by sundown, I shall do as I have said!'

'Very well,' her uncle said, picking up his case, 'but do take care of yourself, my child.'

'I will,' she promised.

'And don't be too emphatic about this

when you report. You'd feel extremely silly if you discovered, after all the fuss, that the young fellow was having a little affair, now, wouldn't you?'

'I'm sure it isn't that,' she protested. She watched her uncle swing away towards the gates, his plump little legs twinkling. When he was out of sight she sat on the veranda, watching the dusty track from the town for some sign of Jack. But the afternoon shadows deepened into evening, and still there was no trace.

As the sun slunk down over the horizon, and darkness gripped the rice fields and tea plantations and cast strange shadows under the pagoda trees, she went into the station to don her coat for the walk into the town. Greatly troubled in her mind, she came out again, made for the steps, then stopped dead.

Two Chinese were coming towards her, whom she knew immediately as the men who had pursued her and Jack that other night. They came straight towards the veranda and paused at the bottom of the steps. Forcing herself to be calm, she said, 'If you wished to see my uncle, he is not here. He has gone to the town which is far away, called Peikan, on matters of some importance.'

The two men smiled, and one of them answered her in Chinese, as she had spoken to him. 'We do not desire to see the white man with the baggy trousers,' he told her. 'It is yourself with whom we have a little business. You will please to come quietly, and not to make any undue disturbance.'

'Come . . . come where?' she stammered.

'That need not concern you at the moment. But come you will, and since there is no need for violence if you act as one with sense, I ask you to accompany us of your own accord.'

'How dare you,' breathed Diana as they came up the steps and took a firm grip of her arms. 'Let me go instantly, or I will scream for help!'

'Scream you may,' commented one of the men, 'but it will merely be a waste of breath. No one could hear you from here, and your first scream would also be your last. I have instructions to use this if necessary!' He took from his pocket a small rubber-covered cosh.

As if she were in some dreadful dream, Diana felt herself guided towards the gate and away from the mission station. Too late she thought of the servants; then she remembered the bamboo splinter which had been stuck into Jack's pillow and wondered if, after all, they also were members of the Tong.

She was led away from the town, along by the deserted rice patches, towards the river. Her captives escorted her onto a small junk, and after they had bound her hands, threw her beneath a mass of dirty sail where she could not be seen by anyone looking in that direction. There were other men on the boat — about three of them. Soon she felt the junk moving away into mid-river, and any hope of escape left her.

It was a horrible journey. For hours and hours they moved silently along, travelling moderately swiftly because of the fresh breeze which was sweeping down from the hills. Faint light seeping in through the canvas which covered her told her dawn had come at last, and stiff and miserable she dropped into uneasy slumber. How long she slept she had no means of knowing, but she was awakened by one of her captors thrusting a hard roll of bread towards her lips.

She shook her head angrily, and was troubled no further. On and on the junk moved, and once again sleep claimed her. When next she woke it was dark again, and the filthy canvas sail had been removed so that fresh air might reach her.

There was a grating noise as the junk ran into a bank, then she was lifted out and laid on the ground. Glancing round she could see they were at a lonely stretch of the river, far down from Liang-Sin. From the junk, two of the sailors produced a collapsible sedan-chair and hastily erected it. Then canvas was stretched over the framework and she was lifted inside. The canvas blotted out her view of the landscape, and she had no idea in which direction they were moving.

Hour after hour it went on: a ceaseless jogging motion. The bearers seemed to be tireless, and their feet covered the ground swiftly, drawing her ever nearer to — what?

Suddenly the sedan was bumped down, and she guessed that they were going to rest. The canvas was drawn aside and she was given some stale food, which she ate this time, her hunger getting the better of her. This was swilled down with a draft of water, and once again she endeavored to question her captors as to where they were taking her. But they merely shook their heads and made no reply.

The wretched journey started again. It went on like that, mile after mile, with occasional rests, until from sheer weariness she fell asleep under the cover of the chair.

But as daylight dawned again, and they stopped for a further break, Diana knew from their remarks that they were nearing their destination. Away in the distance she could distinguish a long line of low hills, bluish coloured in the early morning light. Then the sedan was swung up again, and the party pushed on.

The hills drew steadily nearer, rising straight and sheer into the low clouds over them. The bearers made straight for the foot of them, as if they would climb the sheer rock, sedan and all. But as they approached, Diana could see a cunningly narrow fissure in the hardened earth and stone, and into this they passed. They must have travelled almost a mile more, when the gap ended abruptly. Falling away from them sharply was a long, stony incline leading to a verdant and colorful valley. Away on the far side of the valley could be seen the encircling hills, but what attracted Diana's surprised attention was the temple which stood in the centre of the valley.

Under the first rays of the morning sun it shone with a magnificent lustre; pale gold rays glanced from its terraced pyramidal structure. It was by far the most beautiful, if not the largest, pagoda which the girl had ever seen. Surrounding it were a number of walls built of dark slate-coloured stone. Looking down on it, the girl counted them. There were seven, and involuntarily she gasped as the knowledge came to her: The lost Temple of Confucius!

Without a pause they hurried on through

a verdant wilderness of flowers and shrubs, scent-laden with mimosa plants. The sunlight danced off their delicate yellow blooms, creating a scene which would have thrilled the girl but for the circumstances.

They halted at the first of the thirty-foot-high walls, and one of the men rapped imperatively upon the massive bolt-studded doors. With a great creaking and groaning they swung aside, and the sedan passed in. The same process was repeated seven times, and Diana noted with amazement that strongly armed guards were stationed between each wall.

But at last they were in a wonderful courtyard glittering with the drops of the many fountains which played from its countless pools. It was as if they were in a world apart, a dream world of sunshine and beauty.

The illusion was rapidly dispelled.

The sedan was set down, and roughly the girl was jerked from it. The ropes about her legs were sliced away, and she was lifted to her feet and, being unable to walk, was carried towards the great square doorway leading into the Temple itself.

# 9

## The Lair of the Purple Dragon

Roughly, the gigantic one-eyed Chinaman thrust the bowl of food towards him. Alan took it and began to eat with the spoon which had been provided. It appeared to be a mixture of rice and chopped vegetables, and the American found it not unpalatable.

Chala waited silently until the captive had completed the dish. But his one eye was fixed upon Carrol, and the light which smouldered in it showed that he had not forgotten the kick in the stomach he had received from this man that night long ago when Alan had lost his memory.

The meal completed, Chala took the dish and left the cabin. He was replaced before long by the figure of Lili Lee. She was dressed in coarse Chinese garments as worn by the peasant class, and seemed to be ready for the long journey she had spoken of.

'I fear you will have to walk, Mr. Carrol,' she apologized. 'I do hope you feel fit enough.'

'I will do if I can get the blood circulating in my legs before we start,' he told her calmly.

'But of course! How stupid of me. Chala! Chala!' The giant reappeared. 'Unfasten the bonds about Mr. Carrol's limbs,' she told him.

Grunting a surly reply, the one-eyed monstrosity did so. Then Lili herself helped the American to stand on his numbed legs, and massaged them to encourage circulation.

So close to him, her perfume drifting upwards into his face. Even after what had occurred Alan could still feel that weird fascination which had proved his undoing. With an effort he thrust it into the back of his mind. Lili rose, somewhat flushed. 'There. How's that?'

Alan took a few unsteady steps, groaning with pain as the blood forced a way into his numbed veins. Followed by Lili he stepped out onto the deck and, after a couple of turns up and down, found that he could walk quite easily again.

Glancing towards the banks, he saw something which told him that this whole business had been prearranged. Standing beside a shaded palanquin were four bearers ready to start the journey to the Temple of the Purple Dragon. The party from the sampan disembarked, all except a small man who was staying behind to look after the boat. Lili Lee draped herself elegantly on the palanquin, and Chala fastened a short length of rope round the American's wrists to eliminate any possibility of trickery from that quarter.

Within a few minutes they had started their trek, moving at a slow and regular jog trot directly away from the river bank.

Tied as he was, and with the vicious Chala giving occasional spiteful tugs at the rope which nearly pulled him from his feet, the American found it heavy going. Before they had covered five miles Alan found himself heartily wishing they would halt for a rest. His breath was rasping from his throat, and he had a painful stitch in his side. Also, the effect of the drug he had received had hardly had a chance to wear off.

He found himself eyeing the palanquin bearers with deep envy. They raced on, the sinuous muscles in their legs taut and inexhaustible, their faces blank and expressionless, without a trace of perspiration on them. Alan had often watched the jinrikisha coolies of the big cities pulling a rickshaw containing two plump gentlemen at fast speed for miles. He wondered how on earth they did it on a scanty ration of rice.

He wondered vaguely how Diana and her uncle had taken his disappearance. Of course, he couldn't hope for help from that source, for he had left the note saying he might be away a few days. Possibly they might never bother to wonder what had become of him; would take it for granted he had found out who he really was, and had returned to his old life.

He thought, with something approaching regret, of Diana; he wondered curiously what she would be doing at this moment, and what she would think of him for running out on her. Had he but known it, within the course of forty-eight hours Diana was to be brought over the very route he was finding so tiresome now.

He stumbled along behind the rope which Chala held. His mind began to spin; his entire body ached and pained. He felt desperately ill but doggedly he lurched along, gritting his teeth, determined not to display his weakness.

A loose chunk of stone on the soil was his undoing: his trailing feet knocked against it, and unable to save himself with his hands bound, he crashed helplessly to the ground. Chala snarled at him, dragged him along for a few yards by the rope; he tried to get to his feet, but the fall had wrenched his ankle, and once more he collapsed. Chala stopped, turned, and began to kick him savagely in the stomach.

'Stop that, Chala!' Lili spoke sharply, and the Chinaman sullenly obeyed. Alan scrambled to his feet, and though the ankle almost drove him mad, he began to lope onwards.

'Are you all right, Mr. Carrol?' called the girl.

Face set to hide the pain the movement

was costing him, he nodded. 'If you can slow down a bit I'll manage,' he grunted. But she must have read in his eyes that which he had tried to keep out of his face, for she ordered the coolies to lower her to the ground.

They did so, and quickly she made an examination of the injured ankle. Then she led Alan towards the palanquin and motioned to him to lie on it. Amazed, Alan felt himself gently pushed down, then lifted into the air on the shoulders of the bearers.

Chala growled, 'You let white man *walk*. Him pretend!'

'I saw you pulling that rope, Chala,' she snapped. 'It was as much your doing as his that he tripped up! Now mind your own business, or be sure I will report the matter to the Master.'

The giant relapsed into silence, but his eye flared venomously at the girl, and Alan realized that he hated her.

They got underway again, with Lili trotting at the side of the palanquin. She moved easily and gracefully, and seemed tireless.

Alan thought what a strange woman she was, in some ways. She had administered a drug to him, was taking him to be murdered most likely, and yet she surrendered her comfort and undertook the hardship of a rough journey to save him from some slight pain. He would not have sworn to it, but recently there had been none of the old hate in her eyes, he imagined, and there had even been a little of something else. It seemed that she was beginning to be almost human after all. He wondered if her act when she had coaxed him to the trap had been entirely an act — or if there had been something more to it. Could it be that she was already regretting her part in his downfall?

In spasmodic spells, captive and captors went their way, and after many weary miles came in sight of the Temple of the Purple Dragon. Alan was amazed, as Diana was to be amazed soon after, by the golden magnificence of the ancient temple. It seemed to be almost perfectly preserved. The ravages of time and weather had done little to impair its golden glory; its seven walls stood as stout and straight as they had ever done. And, as one gate after another closed behind them, Alan realized that his chances of escape or rescue from this place were absolutely nil.

At one of the fountains in the courtyard, Lili halted the party. Removing a loose sash from her waist, she dipped it in the cool water, drew Alan's sock down, and bound his ankle with it. As she did so she averted her gaze from his eyes, ignoring his low, 'Thanks; I'll do the same for you someday, maybe.'

Now he was helped from the palanquin and half-carried towards the door to the temple proper. On either side of the door stood a huge guard clad in a leather and brass harness. Each bore a heavy curved ceremonial sword, whether for effect or purpose was uncertain, but Alan imagined the former, since no one could have possibly penetrated so far past the walls.

Somewhere within the pagoda a gong boomed, and immediately the double doors swung majestically aside to admit the weary travellers.

Within, all was shrouded in gloom; but as his eyes became accustomed to the darkness, Alan could discern a vast and high chamber lined with figures and statues carved in pagodite. His nose detected the scent of burning lotus leaves, sweet and sickly, rising from two censers which hung before a marble altar at the far end of the chamber.

Beyond them, carved from what appeared to be wood, and with a massive, open, tooth-studded jaw, rested a painted Purple Dragon. It was fully fifty feet in length, and almost ten feet high. The barbs and spikes along its spine stood out sharply, realistically; its trident-shaped tail swept impressively upwards towards the high dome of the ceiling.

Without being allowed more than a brief glance at this, Alan was dragged towards an ornate circular staircase to one side of the temple. Lili leading, they progressed up the stairs, and along a wide corridor wrapped in gloom and redolent of long-burned incense. The Chinese girl threw open a door on the right and said: 'Your apartment, Mr. Carrol. I trust you will be comfortable . . . I will bring you food later. First of all, though, I think you will have a little visit from Yatso Lan Oh, who acts as high priest of our little circle.'

'Tell me,' said Alan, curiosity overcoming despair, 'why do you bother to keep up the pretence of the Purple Dragon Tong, even to having a high priest?'

She smiled and said, 'You see, Mr. Carrol, although people such as you and I, and some of our more educated Tongmen, do not believe in all this hokum, the more uneducated of our members still do. The outlaws, bandits and pirates who roam the hills and rivers, and who periodically bring their loot here to be stored, believe very deeply in all this. So deeply, in fact, that they would never dare to disobey any commands issued by the officiating priests. They understand that the Master is omnipotent, knows all things. To foster their fear, human sacrifices have been arranged from time to time — traitors, enemies, anyone the Tong wishes to dispose of. By that means we keep the natives in continual dread.'

113

Chala chuckled evilly, having picked up the trend of the conversation. 'And you be one for sacrifice, Carrol!'

Lili frowned and snapped, 'Leave us, Chala!'

Surlily the one-eyed sadist did as he was bid. The door closed behind him, and Lili walked over to the young American. 'Mr. Carrol, if you will give me your promise not to start anything, I am willing to remove the bonds from your wrists.'

'Okay, you've got it! Wouldn't be much sense in starting anything, anyway. I'd never be able to finish it.'

Quickly she untied him, then retired to the door again. She said, 'I shall have to lock you in — but I think Yatso Lan Oh will be here to speak with you before you have a chance to get bored. *Au revoir*, for now.'

She left the room, and Alan heard the key twist in the lock behind her. Then he was alone in a chamber in the Lair of the Purple Dragon.

# 10

## Opium

It could hardly have been an hour after Lili Lee had left the room before Alan heard the sound of a key grating in the lock again, and the door reopened.

There was a Chinaman standing there: a tall, thin, cruel-lipped man with eyes which slanted excessively. Alan gained the impression that he had seen the fellow before — but where and when he had no notion. The Chinaman, who was attired in a dragon-embroidered robe, walked with small, shuffling steps into the room, closing the door behind him. Alan turned from the large iron-barred opening in the wall from which he had been gazing down onto the scene beneath.

The Chinaman said, 'Mr. Carrol, of course. I am Yatso Lan Oh.'

'Sit down,' said Alan. 'Miss Lee told me you would be coming.'

The priest smiled. He said, 'A charming girl, Miss Lee. So efficient — and such a clever father . . . '

'I'm afraid I haven't the pleasure of knowing Mr. Lee,' Alan told him.

'Mr. Lee? Oh, but of course! A natural mistake to make. Lee is not the girl's father's name. It is her mother's, I believe. I'm afraid her parents weren't married, Mr. Carrol. But we are broad-minded men, and such a thing implies no stigma, does it?'

Alan felt his cloak of nonchalance beginning to desert him. He was trying to affect indifference to the reason for the high priest's visit, but the aggravating way the man had of talking all round a subject before actually coming to the point irritated him. He had found it to be a trait of many Chinese since he had left the hospital.

'Yes, a very natural mistake,' continued Yatso Lan Oh, 'but there is no reason for you to continue to labour under the assumption that Miss Lee's father was named Lee also. Her father is a very clever European — in fact, an Englishman. He is the brains behind our little organization, the ruler of the Purple Dragon Tong.'

'He must indeed be clever.'

'Yes, yes, of course.' Yatso lit a thin cigarette, then offered the case to Alan. Alan shook his head. 'I suppose you have a good idea why I am here? You will no doubt have formed your opinions of what must inevitably happen to those who know too much concerning our little organization?'

'I have. I presume I will be murdered,' said Alan, a trifle grimly.

'How naïve you are, Mr. Carrol! You presume you will be murdered! But *of course* you will — however, let us not call it murder. Let us rather say sacrificed for the benefit of our members.'

'Is there a difference?'

'Not from your point of view, of course, but there is from ours — definitely.'

'Sacrificed or murdered, what does it matter what we call it?' said Alan. 'It boils down to the same thing — except that your method will probably take a little longer than outright murder.'

'You are right, Mr. Carrol — it will take

considerably longer.'

'I imagined so.'

'How refreshingly enchanting,' said the high priest, 'to meet a man who can discuss his own — er — demise so calmly and without rancour.'

'Would it make any difference if I betrayed my real feelings?'

'No, no, I fear not.'

'Then what purpose would hysteria serve?'

'You know, Mr. Carrol, you are an unusual man. No doubt you would like to know exactly why you must die. I take it you have not yet regained your memory?'

'If I am to die I don't know that I am very interested in the reasons — but since it will help to pass the time until my . . . '

'Execution!' suggested the priest.

'Execution,' Alan acknowledged. 'By all means, tell me.'

Yatso Lan Oh settled himself more comfortably and smoothed down his robe. He said, 'It happened about — oh, eight months ago. We, having the advantage of knowing just who you are, have made enquiries — very discreet, of course — into your background, and have found out why you were in Liang-Sin, when no Europeans were supposed to be in the town at that time.

'It seems that you were a reporter stationed in Chungking — a foreign correspondent for the American newspaper, *The Daily Recorder*. But you found life too tame there: there was no opportunity of getting a scoop, as you term it, for your paper.

'It came to your ears that there were strange activities going on in Liang-Sin, which was much nearer to the front line and which, it was understood, the Japanese would reach with their next big push. So without any permission you sneaked into Liang-Sin one evening, eight months ago.

'You were fortunate! You had been there only a week when your enquiries reached the ears of one of our men who had failed to perform a task we had set him to our satisfaction, and who must die accordingly. He came to you at night and offered you the information he had regarding our activities, for enough money to get him far away from Liang-Sin. You accepted!

'Unfortunately for you and your

informant, you were both unaware that he was being watched. Therefore, we had no difficulty in securing you both and taking you to our headquarters in Liang-Sin.

'There, you enjoyed the spectacle of watching our traitor tortured rather nastily. But before we could arrive at you, you managed to escape. In the subsequent pursuit you were blown up by a Japanese bomb and we, thinking you had been killed, were content.

'But as time went by it was discovered that there was an unknown American in the hospital, delirious and suffering from a bad case of prolonged concussion. We waited, biding our time, until you came out. And then the Master himself recognized you, and your fate was sealed. Now you understand all?'

'All except one thing: what was the information which I held, which caused you so much uneasiness? And why bother to kill me if I had lost my memory?'

'In answer to your first question, the information you held would have been sufficient to have had us all stood before a firing squad, had it been revealed. There is no reason to keep you in the dark any longer, Mr. Carrol. So I will tell you: you had not only learned the names of the top six leaders of the Tong, but you had also learned of our plans to assist the Japanese!'

'Collaborators!'

'Collaborators, Fifth Columnists, call it what you will. We prefer to owe allegiance to no country, but we recently had some trouble with the Chinese government. In fact, soldiers were sent to wipe us out. They caught only the small fry, but naturally we were somewhat annoyed.'

'You have a positive gift for understatement,' said Alan.

'Have I? Well, perhaps we were really angry then. So it was arranged between ourselves and a certain gentleman who acts as an agent for the Japanese military that we should prepare to hand over the town to them when they came and, if necessary, to help them in any way possible. The defeat of the Japanese Army put an end to that, of course, but on finding you were still alive and had information which would have caused us

121

much trouble — I believe they are now shooting collaborators. If that information became known . . . That made it essential to bring your life here to an end.

'You had lost your memory, yes! But there was no saying at what minute you might regain it! Do you still remember nothing?'

'I'm not so sure,' said Alan, wrinkling his brow. 'I seem to recall most of what you say — in a hazy kind of way, though.'

'Good, good! Now you know why you must die. I trust you think we are justified in sacrificing you?'

'Possibly from your own point of view,' said Alan, nodding. 'Tell me one more thing: who is the Master?'

Yatso Lan Oh shook his head regretfully and rose from his seat. He crossed towards the door and opened it. He said, 'I am not at liberty to tell you that, I fear. However, you will see him yourself before you meet your end. And he was in that cellar the night we — er — executed Lin See. Perhaps if you strain your memory . . .'

'I'm afraid not. I can't seem to recollect any of the men in that cellar. But I'm obliged to you for telling me what I was, if for nothing else.'

'You have two more days of life, as yet,' said the priest with a smile. 'You will be well treated here if you act in a seemly manner.'

'And what is a seemly manner for a condemned man to act in?'

Yatso Lan Oh smiled again and withdrew.

For a long time Alan sat and mused over the things he had been told. Now that his adventures prior to his loss of memory had been clarified, he seemed to remember, vaguely, the events which Yatso had spoken of. But he was still unable to bring to mind the names or faces of the men who had been in that cellar the night of his misadventure. He sat for hours lost in thought, but finally his mind turned to his more immediate necessities. Die he might, but while he lived he needed food; and Lili, who had promised to send some along to him, appeared to have forgotten.

He crossed to the window again, stiffened, and stared down in quickly kindled curiosity. Down below, walking rapidly across the courtyard, was a man in European garb. There seemed something faintly familiar about his gait, but he was gone too quickly for Alan to glimpse more than the top of his hat.

The turning of the key in the lock brought him round to face the door again, in the hope that this might be food at last.

He was not disappointed. Chala entered, followed by Lili. Chala bore a tray on which, Alan saw, reposed various Chinese dishes in thin, wafer-like China bowls and plates. He crossed towards Alan and stood in front of him, holding the tray towards him.

'Why we feed *this* prisoner?' he grunted sourly. His eye bore the glazed look of the opium smoker, and Alan judged he had been on the pipe since he had last been there.

Lili answered in a curt tone, 'I've warned you, Chala, to mind your own business. You have too much to say when you've been taking opium. Now give Mr. Carrol the tray.'

'Yah!' said the lumbering native, grinning malignantly. 'I give him the tray!' And with a sudden movement he shot the tray and its contents into Alan's features.

It was too much! Scarcely had the dishes crashed floorwards, than Alan sunk his fist hard into the giant's diaphragm. Chala, not expecting this treatment from a defenceless prisoner, doubled up in agony. He drew in great, sucking breaths.

'My God!' gasped Lili from the door — and it sounded strangely unreal to hear that phrase from *her* lips. 'You — you shouldn't have done that! He's been opium-smoking, and he's a devil at these times . . . '

Alan backed cautiously away from the one-eyed Chala as he gasped and panted for air. Slowly Chala recovered and came upright. His eye fixed on Alan with a dreadful intensity, glassy but murderous. Like an automaton he began to advance towards the American, hands formed in cruel claws, face still blank and idiotic.

Lili ran across the room and threw herself in front of him. She screamed, 'No, Chala! The Master will kill you if you harm this man — he is for sacrifice, understand. Get back, Chala! Back!'

Chala did not speak. He seized the girl in one tremendous hand and flung her violently out of his path. She crashed into a chair, sprawled on the floor.

'Kill!' hissed Chala malevolently. Inexorably he came round the table and edged towards Alan, who was trapped in a corner.

'Chala — kill!'

Then he was on the American. He picked him up in a mighty grip and sent him hurling across the room, to smash into the far wall. He leaped over towards the dazed American, following up his advantage by thrusting a mighty arm round his throat, squeezing.

But now Lili was back, armed with a bamboo chair, her face taut and grim. She smashed blow after blow down on the insensate giant; suddenly he snarled and allowed Alan to slide to the floor, then turned on the slender girl. His hand reached out for her and ripped the kimono she wore from neckline to waist. Her olive body was revealed to his eye, and the malice turned to sudden lust; he came towards her as she backed for the door. As she reached out to find the handle, his long arm swept out and pulled her, screaming, towards him. Weird slobbering cries emerged from his blubbery lips, and the worms of desire crawling in that one eye belied the putty-like insensibility of his features. His hand ran along the girl's body; she shuddered away from the touch of it and tried to break loose. Her fingernails scored deep red furrows in his face. With an oath, Chala struck her a heavy blow in the mouth; red blood spurted from between her red lips. And then he was carrying her, half-dazed, to the divan.

Alan, coming dimly back to consciousness, was aware of the monstrous figure kneeling over the half-nude form on the divan. His eyes darted frantically about for some means of saving the girl — and they fell on the long silken drapes, secured by a thin silken cord.

Chala, intent on this new game of his, knew nothing until the cord settled tightly about his throat, and then he went berserk. He thrashed about the room, roaring, screaming maniacally. His flailing arms semaphored wild punches, some of which struck Alan; but the American held on, even when the giant rolled on top of him, battering at his face. He felt the hot blood spurt from his smashed teeth and lips, but with a grim relentlessness he hung on, tightening the cord with each fresh struggle Chala attempted.

And slowly, gradually, Chala's struggles weakened. His roars dropped to throaty gurgles; his long, dough-like tongue whipped despairingly between his thick lips . . . His arms dropped limply to the floor.

Alan glanced towards Lili, now sitting up, watching the scene with passionate anger blazing from her dark eyes. He said, 'I think he's senseless now.'

Her voice came back, harsh and cold: 'Kill him! It is not safe for either of us if he lives!'

'But . . . '

'Are you afraid? He is but scum!'

She was right; Chala would never forget this. Closing his mind to his actions, Alan tightened the cord still further.

When he rose, Chala lay still, his one

eye fixed and glaring blankly, lifelessly, up at the ceiling. Alan wiped the sweat from his brow and shook his head.

'Do not worry over him,' said Lili, the harshness gone from her voice. 'He would have killed us both!'

'I guess that wouldn't have made much difference to me — it would probably have been quicker than the death your pals have in store for me, at any rate,' he replied bitterly.

A look of pain shot into the girl's eyes. She ignored the remark and said, 'I will have him removed.' She pulled down one of the curtains and wound it round her body to conceal herself. She crossed to the door, picked up the key from where it had fallen, opened the door and called, 'Sing Yan — Le Ling!'

Two servants answered her call, and she motioned them into the room. She said, 'Remove this carrion!'

Their inscrutable faces betrayed no surprise. An onlooker would have obtained the idea that it was part of the day's routine to carry away strangled bodies. Alan gained that impression.

Lili Lee turned back towards the American. She said, 'Thank you for saving my worthless life' in Chinese. Her eyes were troubled as she closed the door, and once again Alan was locked in.

He tried to bathe his cut mouth with a piece of Lili's torn kimono, which he dipped in the tea on the floor. He didn't feel so hungry now. It was just as well.

He sat down with his head in his hands. He wished he had let Chala finish him off, but for the girl. No matter what she had done, he could not have stood by and watched any brute like Chala maul a woman. He cursed himself for a quixotic fool. He knew that strangulation would have been infinitely preferable to the fate in store for him.

And he knew that Lili had done nothing but trap him into this filthy position. And yet, the little things she had done to comfort his last hours: the surrendering of the palanquin to him, the bandaging of his ankle, the fight she had put up with Chala . . . No, he didn't regret his action after all.

She was a strange creature, this

half-caste girl whose father was head of the Purple Dragon Tong. She could see a man killed mercilessly before her eyes — even wish his death without a shiver. And yet, her standards were not the standards of the West. Her whole life, upbringing, was as far removed from Diana's as the earth from the sun. And there must still be much good in her — she had betrayed herself at times.

But he was her father's enemy, and as such, must be ruthlessly eliminated. No matter how she felt about it, her Chinese blood, coupled with her way of life, must prevail. Her father, to her, was the giver-of-laws, the master of her destiny. Thus it was, Alan thought, with all true Chinese. They were ruled in the present by their parents, from the past by their ancestors; and the ways of their ancestors, and the laws which their ancestors laid down.

He shrugged, smiled a little, crossed over to the bars and gazed down into the courtyard. He could hear the mighty gates in the walls being opened and shut one after the other. Someone was coming.

He fixed his gaze upon the last gate, watched it open, and saw the covered sedan brought in.

He saw it halt, watched a girl lifted out . . . and then his face was transformed into a horrified mask and he called wildly, *'Diana!'*

The girl glanced up, her terrified eyes met his, and then she was dragged from his sight.

# 11

## Meet the Master!

After that one despairing glimpse of the man she knew as Jack Green, Diana was dragged inside the Temple. Hopelessly she took in the details of the altar room, the painted dragon. With an awful finality she realized that the altar in front of that dragon was used for sacrifice — human sacrifice!

She had, as yet, no clear idea why she had been captured and brought here; she imagined that in some way the gang had come to hear of her proposed visit to the authorities. Possibly one of the servants at the mission had been listening when she had told her uncle what she intended to do. She thought of the reverend with a kind of sickness: he was far away, and she wondered how he would take it when he returned and found her gone. Not that he had ever shown much affection for her.

He had looked upon it as his duty to look after her, more or less, and she had been a good housekeeper for him. No, certainly he couldn't feel any real grief.

Hardly knowing where she was taken, she at last found herself in a small room similar to the one Alan was in. There was the barred window space and a divan, nothing more. Her hands were untied and she flung herself wearily down onto the divan. As the door shut behind her captors, tears sprung to her eyes and she sobbed bitterly — not only for the predicament she herself was in, but also for Jack. She had realized, these last twenty-four hours, how much she thought of him; and seeing him behind those bars with his mouth stained with blood, as if he had been through unimaginable terrors, she knew that she actually loved him!

Food was brought to her after a while, and she brushed away her tears and tried to eat. But the food stuck in her throat, and finally she pushed it away largely untouched.

With the servant who came to clear the plates, came someone else. She was standing with her back to the window at the time and did not realize that there was anyone there until the servant had left. Then her senses impressed upon her that she was not alone. She turned to see her visitor, and at the sight of him a sob of joy left her lips:

'Uncle!'

But although the man standing there was undeniably the Reverend Harper, there was a look about his face which she had never seen before. And as the question of what he was doing here asserted itself in her mind, her face blanched and she took a backward step.

'Yes, Diana,' he said impassively, 'it's your uncle, all right. And very sorry to see you in this situation. You know that you are going to die, don't you?'

'I — I don't understand,' she faltered.

'Oh, come now!' he said impatiently. 'Didn't I warn you when I left the station that it was unwise to meddle with the affairs of Tongs and Societies? I could scarcely do more! But you persisted in your foolish determination to put Carrol's disappearance before the authorities, and

135

there was no alternative but to have you brought here. I could, of course, have had you eliminated on the spot, but that would have caused too many questions to have been asked.'

'Carrol?' said the girl, seizing on the name. 'Who — who's Carrol?'

'Carrol is your Jack Green. He knows a little too much about us — as do you. Since you are obviously rather attached to him, it may comfort you to know that you will both die within a few hours of each other.'

'You *beast!*' gasped the girl. 'So you never intended to go into the interior? You never have been! Each time you've said you were going to some other station you've actually been *here!*'

'Quite correct.'

'How could you work with a gang like this? I always thought you so good and kind . . . And now I find you're a member of a murderous society . . . '

'Member? My dear child, you humiliate me. *I am the Master!*'

'So it was *you* who put the poisoned needle in Jack's — I mean Carrol's bed?'

'It was. Incidentally, my child, Carrol's first name is Alan. I'm sure he'd like you to use his first name. Carrol sounds so formal, don't you think?'

'But why . . . why have you done all this?'

'A tedious story, child. However, if you wish . . . It started twenty-five years ago. I had been out five years then, and I was young and rather foolish. In spite of my exalted station I fell in love with a Chinese girl. Of course it was out of the question that I should *marry* her — but unfortunately she bore me a child. She died in childbirth — the mother, Laing Lee — but the child survived. Imagine it: *me* a missionary, with a child born *illegitimately* of a Chinese mother!

'I needed money to send her away; I was determined to give her everything else, if she could not have a father. And I started this little game. But the power I wielded went to my head, I admit it frankly. It was more money, more money, all the time! Long after my daughter returned from America I went on, until this very day — and I will continue to run

this Tong long after it. Now you understand why you must die. And your friend,
Alan Carrol, must die also.'

'Get *out*,' sobbed Diana wildly. 'Leave
me alone!'

She heard the door close but she did
not look up. Her tears fell unheeded on to
the silken cover of the divan.

# 12

## Human Sacrifice

Diana received no further visitors for almost twenty-four hours. After a time her tears dried, and she fell into a sleep of pure exhaustion.

When she awoke, she became aware of a ceaseless babble from the direction of the courtyard. Looking from her window, she saw thin lines of Chinamen clad in the rough irregular mode of dress affected by hill bandits and junk pirates. Many of them bore old-fashioned carbines and heavy pistols; some sported a long sword driven through their belt; and one or two, at least, were equipped with the latest thing in modern rifling. They created a picturesque sight with their broad bandoliers strapped about their shoulders and hooked onto their belts; but Diana saw them with a sense of horror, for it was obvious they had come here to witness the deaths of herself and Alan.

Meanwhile, in his prison room farther along, Alan, too, watched the arrival of the ruffian band. There were men of all types: from the hills, from the cities, from the riverbanks. Men who had fled justice, traitors, renegades, and a smattering of Mongol types from beyond the Great Wall. He knew a kind of sick despair as he watched them enter, for he, too, realized that this indicated the time was near. He thought about Diana; he guessed from the way she had been dragged in that she, too, was a captive, and was likely to meet with the same punishment as himself.

So, not twenty feet from each other, yet unable to speak. Diana and Alan awaited their deaths.

Diana knew that she was to die first; her uncle had told her that. But how long?

From the main hall of the temple below drifted up the noise of a large gathering of people. After a time the noise was stilled, and high and clear in the now-hushed temple rose the monotonous chanting of a high priest. Evening was drawing on, and behind the walls of the far hills the red-streaked sun was gradually setting in a blaze of glory — setting for the two captives for the last time, and they both watched it with mixed feelings.

Shortly, the sound of the single chant died away, and all the gathering lifted up their voices in subdued worship. The swelling chanted chorus rang through the temple, gathered volume, and caromed from the arched ceiling in an unreal mélange of sound. Then it died away again, and the voice of the high priest became audible, continuing the chant alone.

Two kimonoed women entered Diana's room, bearing jars of oil and a highly flowered robe. Not unkindly, they commenced to strip the girl, who stood there cold and trembling, not caring much what happened now her death was so close. Rapidly they anointed her quivering suntanned limbs with the scented oils they bore, then helped her into the flowered robe.

'What — what will happen to — to me?' asked the girl.

'Little sun-brown sister,' replied one of the women gravely, 'you have been chosen for a great honour! It is the time of the Bride of the Dragon Festival, and you are to be the bride! Is that not a great honour?'

Diana laughed bitterly. The woman was deadly serious, and Diana wondered how such superstitious nonsense could still exist in the heart of twentieth-century China. 'But what will happen to me?' she persisted.

'You will be placed upon the Tongue of the Dragon. The high priest will pronounce blessings upon you, and then the Dragon's jaws will close. After that nothing will be heard but your screams!'

'Screams? Does a bride usually scream?'

'Some brides do,' stated the woman, being unintentionally ironic. 'And more especially, the brides of the Dragon. It is said that they scream with ecstasy — be that as it may, they are never seen again.'

The idea of what might happen when the jaws of that wooden dragon closed sent Diana into a fit of shuddering.

'See,' said the Chinese woman to her

companion. 'She trembles with the intoxication of the delights to come!'

They made the final adjustments to her robe, opened the door and led her outside. Here there waited a golden painted sedan chair and two bearers clad in flowing robes. A fit carriage for the bride of the Dragon!

The two bearers, probably priests, slipped silver chains about the girl's wrists and ankles. The chains were drawn tight, then locked. She was lifted into the sedan, and the procession prepared to move off. But now they were joined by others, carrying cymbals and reed flutes. The bride of the Dragon was going to have music for her nuptials. Pageantry, ceremony.

Diana thought it was more of a funeral procession than anything else, as indeed it was.

They proceeded to the top of the staircase and waited. The sounds of chanting below had died away with one tremendous shout. And, echoing unnervingly in the gloom and silence of that ancient Temple of Confucius, came the solitary note of a brassy gong.

As it reverberated about the walls the cavalcade began to move down the stairs, setting up a wailing chant, beating the cymbals, and producing the thin, oppressed warbling of reed flutes.

Gradually the main hall of worship came into view, its serried ranks of disreputables straining their eyes to catch a glimpse of the chosen woman who was betrothed to the Purple Dragon. In the sedan Diana sat still and silent, crushing back the fear which bade her kick and scream; beating down the wild, unbearable panic which tore at her mind and limbs. If she must die, she would at least die bravely.

Down the centre aisle they went, the sedan borne slowly past the rows of brutal faces, flushed with the worship throes of a wooden god. A pathetic, foolish thought flashed through Diana's mind. If only this were a proper church, and that Alan was by her side!

The procession halted reverently at the foot of the steps leading up to the Dragon. Here, a group of priests in purple robes stood before the crowd; but looking at their faces, Diana could see that they, at least, believed only in the Dragon as a method of terrifying and subjecting their followers. Indeed, one or two she recognized as prominent men in Liang-Sin and its surrounding territories.

Her uncle, now attired in rich purple robes, stood upon the highest step, and just beneath him stood a cruel-lipped Chinese whom she knew as Yatso Lan Oh, a tea merchant. There was no sign of recognition in his face as she was lifted down from the sedan.

Four of the priests moved silently forward to receive her; she was borne slowly up the steps to the small platform before the Dragon's mouth. Inside the mouth, between the twin rows of painted wooden fangs, there was a forked red tongue. Upon this she was gently laid, and the priests retired to their positions. As the chanting swelled up once more, now with a jubilant note, Diana said a small prayer that she might not gratify their desire to hear her scream whatever happened to her. Then the brazen tone of the gong clamoured again through the place, above the chanting of the worshippers, and the chant was cut off abruptly.

She gazed down towards her uncle, but his head was averted; she looked out on the mass of Tongmen thronging the hall; their mouths were gaping with a tense expectancy. To her, all eternity seemed to be crammed into those few silent seconds. And then the massive upper jaw snapped shut, a great wail rose from the worshippers, and the forked tongue on which she reposed tilted suddenly. She felt herself sliding rapidly, madly, downwards, down a black tunnel to . . . She set her lips grimly and prepared to die without a sound . . .

In the temple, the worshippers still gazed fanatically at the closed mouth of the Dragon. They were waiting for the scream, the agonized scream which would tell them that all was over and that the Dragon had received his bride.

And at last it came, shrill and throbbing! The jaws of the idol opened once more, and welling up from them came the voice of a girl, unmistakably Diana's, screaming in unendurable agony . . .

# 13

## The Way of the East

The steady, rising chanting from the temple was getting on Alan Carrol's nerves. Torn by the fearful anxiety of what might be happening to Diana, he paced the prison chamber in a burst of savage impotency. His hands clenched as he thought of the cold, ruthless features of Yatso Lan Oh; Diana could expect no mercy from that quarter.

Unaware that Diana was in the room next but one to him, he crossed to the window and gazed out upon the crimson splendour of the setting sun. The knowledge that Diana was faced with a shocking death unnerved him and made him think of her more intently; and slowly came the realization that whereas his feelings for Lili Lee had been only of passion and desire, his feelings for Diana were of love.

But now it was too late. Soon — perhaps within the next few hours — he would be gone, and Diana also.

He was brought from these unpleasant reflections by a soft step in the room, and turning he beheld Lili, who had entered unheard.

She was once again dressed in European clothing, and looked as she had that night he had first met her. As he spun round, she placed a finger to her lips warningly and said, 'I am not supposed to be here — do not make too much noise!'

'Of course you're not,' grunted Alan impatiently. 'Why the hell don't you get into your ceremonial robes and beat it downstairs with the rest of those chanting bastards?'

He saw Lili wince at the word, and did not know how much he had hurt her by its use. She said, 'I came to — to . . .'

'To gloat? Well, go right ahead! Gloat away, sister! Help yourself — it's the last chance you'll get to gloat over me! But surely your pals will miss you at the ceremony?'

'No. I do not like to go to these affairs . . .'

'Well,' mocked Alan, 'you don't tell me? I should have thought you were callous enough for anything.'

And then, before he had any idea of what was happening, she flung herself towards him, wrapping her arms about his neck and clinging, with pulsating body pressed hard against him.

'Oh, Alan,' she said, half-sobbing. 'I — I love you! I know now . . . '

He pushed her roughly away. He said bitingly, 'Is this one more of your damned tricks?'

'No — no, Alan, I swear it! I know I trapped you, deceived you, but . . . I didn't know you then. I thought you were a weak fool . . . '

'And what's convinced you that I'm not?'

'I don't know — just little things . . . Your ankle, the way you tried to walk with it . . . The way you talked after you had found out I had drugged you. Perhaps the way you turned against me; but in spite of that you fought with Chala to save me from — from . . . '

'Don't remind me of that! I'm almost

regretting it, since I saw that girl brought here! You're as much to blame as your father for all this.'

'But I'm not, Alan. I didn't know what was happening until I returned from America, after I had been through college. Honestly! And Father did all this for me; what could I do but help?'

'I suppose you're proud to have an organization like this operating, so that you can have ease and luxury?'

'No — not now, Alan. After you killed Chala for me I went back to my room and tried to think. I remembered all they taught me in America, and what it meant. I still love my father. I can't blame him for what he's done, and will do, but I know now that what I learned over there was right, and that what my father's doing is wrong!'

'I'd like to believe that,' said Alan.

'But you can believe it! I swear it. I told you once before that I couldn't make you understand the way of the East. But I can understand the way of the West — I was blinding myself to it until you fought with Chala . . . and then, it all came back! No

Easterner would fight like that to save a woman he must hate, a woman who had trapped him into becoming a condemned man. But you did, and I knew then that the ways of the West were, if not wise, gallant and fair. I found that the Western side of me, which I had tried so hard to subdue, was stronger than the Eastern side!'

'Swell! That's all very nice to know, Lili, but what does it get me? You're a bit too late, I guess. And what's happening to the girl they brought here — Diana Harper?'

A strange look came into Lili's eyes. She said, 'You — you love this girl?'

'I guess I do!'

'But — I thought that you — you might love me? I can show you what it means to love, better than that pale, insignificant, strait-laced Englishwoman.'

'All I *ever* felt for you, Lili, was just infatuation! That's all I *ever* could feel for you — we're poles apart!'

She drew back from his arms suddenly. Her face blazed. 'So! Perhaps you did not know that I came here to help you to

151

escape? But now I will let you die — I will *watch* you die! And I will laugh — laugh as you writhe and twist under the sacrificial knife! When they lay you on the altar and strike, I will spit upon you!'

'Hello!' Alan grinned without mirth. 'I see you aren't so far from your Eastern standard after all! And, in any case, I wouldn't care to escape without Diana!'

Lili's eyes blazed at him. She snapped, 'Do you know what will happen to your precious Diana? Do you know what will become of her; the agony she will go through before death claims her? You think she will die under the knife, but no! Her death will be worse than that, I assure you!

'She is to be the bride of the Dragon. She will be placed upon the Dragon's tongue, the jaws will close, and she will slide down a narrow, dark tunnel to a chamber beneath the floor of the temple. Beneath the opening through which she will come, bound with strong chains, there are fifty steel spikes. She will fall upon these from a height of ten feet; they will impale her, stab through her frail

152

body, torturing her with a million deaths before the true death claims her!

'It is seldom, very seldom, that one of the spikes pierces a vulnerable part, and so brings death instantly. And while she lies screaming and squirming in agony, they, up in the Temple, will hear her shrieks, jubilantly. And then they will chant again, and it will be two hours before they come to kill you! Two weary hours, during which time you will have the solace of knowing your loved one lies bleeding and impaled upon the spikes down there, dying by inches. At least, your end will be quicker. Your torture lasts only fifteen minutes, perhaps less, and then — the final stroke! But she — Diana — will lie there bleeding . . . '

'Damn you, shut up!' rasped Alan, and his hand connected squarely with her face.

She took a step backward, her hand flying to her cheek. Her eyes flamed at him, and he watched her carefully, half-expecting her to draw a knife on him. But what happened was entirely different, and something for which he was utterly

153

unprepared. With a heart-wrenching sob, Lili threw herself on the divan, her body shaking with misery.

For some moments Alan watched her in silence. This was no act; it was too real for that. Sudden compassion seized him; after all, he thought, this girl was different. And there was a saying: Hell hath no fury . . . He walked across to her and sat down by her side. Gently he raised her tear-stained face, his hand under her chin. He grinned encouragingly, wiping her cheeks with his handkerchief. She sniffed and fingered the tears from the corners of her eyes. 'You — you are very mad at me, Alan?'

'No, I guess not. I like you, somehow . . . and I reckon you don't really know what you're saying when you're mad. It's the vindictive blood in you, I suppose, which causes you to revert to the ways of your people.'

Lili stood up. Her face shone with a great decision. 'Alan. I will prove to you that I can overcome that strain! Listen: I will help you to escape — you and your . . . girlfriend.'

'You mean that? No fooling?'

'I mean it — but we must hurry! Already the first gong has sounded, and the second denotes the moment of sacrifice. Quickly, follow me!'

Hastily she led him out of the room, listening for a second to the chanting from below. She said, 'We have just a minute or two!'

Then they were racing along the passage, away from the main hall. Down a flight of steps she led him, along a short corridor; they came to a halt beside a door at the far end, and Lili fumbled desperately with a key which she unhooked from a chain about her neck. The door opened with its aid, and they broke into a cellar.

It was bristling with armaments of every description, both old and new. Boxes of ammunition and cases of dynamite were discernible by the rays of a lamp which stood in the room beyond and cast a pallid glow through the square hole in the stonework. And then they were through and into the inner chamber, which plain and unfurnished. The glimmering lamp revealed, to one side, a narrow tunnel about ten feet from the floor; and beneath it, spreading for a matter of ten feet in a square, even pattern, were fifty steel spikes, two feet high and glistening where the light of the lamp fell upon them.

And as they broke through the square aperture, from somewhere above a gong sounded dully!

# 14

## The Man Who Found Himself

For perhaps a second they stood petrified. Then Lili gasped, 'Quick, Alan! You can just about get your feet between the spikes — try to get under the mouth of the tunnel, and catch her! In just a second she will slide down . . . '

Moving faster than he could ever recall moving before, Alan hastily threaded his way through the cruel spikes; they were razor-sharp along the edges also, and his shoes were ripped and sliced as his feet crushed against them. But at last he was under the tunnel, tensing himself to catch Diana.

And she came! She came swiftly, eyes closed, lips set, plunging helplessly down to her doom.

The impact of her body staggered Alan, and, for a moment, he thought he would crash down under her weight. But two hands braced against his back, and he knew that Lili was there also.

Diana opened her eyes as she felt the strong arms about her, and wonder shone from her face. Lili said quickly, '*Scream!* Scream as if you were in agony, or they will suspect and we will be discovered!'

Diana rapidly grasped her command and the cause for it, and opening her mouth she delivered a series of wild, throbbing shrieks.

She continued to do so as they picked their way from the spikes, and as Lili and Alan worked desperately to ease the chains from her wrists and ankles. After a while she permitted her screams to die away into prolonged moaning, and from above came a renewed burst of chanting.

'They are preparing for the sacrifice of the man now,' Lili said briskly. 'Come with me and I will take you out of this place.'

'But how? How on earth can we hope to get past seven walls, each one patrolled by sentries?' said Alan, puzzled.

'There is no necessity to do that. In this chamber there is a secret tunnel which runs beneath the ground, under the walls, and comes out fifty yards away from the temple.'

'But when they find out I am missing,' exclaimed Alan, 'they will pursue me! And what chance have I against a horde like those?'

Lili said, 'Very little! But you must take your chances of escaping. There are plenty of spots in which to hide in this valley, and you can gradually work your way towards them, until you have thrown off pursuit. I cannot help you further. When you are gone I must return, and if you escape I must help my father to leave this place before the military investigate your information.'

She was pressing a section of the stone wall, and a three-foot block suddenly swung open, revealing the interior of a dark passage.

'Take Diana,' exclaimed Alan suddenly. 'I will follow. I wish to provide myself with weapons from the armory there.'

'Hurry!' cautioned Lili, and pressed on into the secret exit. Alan turned back into the storeroom, and after the interval of a minute reappeared. He seized the oil lamp hanging in the inner chamber and vanished once more.

Finally, he rushed out and down the escape tunnel, two neat revolvers clutched in his hands.

For a matter of twenty-five yards the tunnel sloped rapidly. Then it commenced to rise, and a patch of daylight became visible in the gloom. Alan burst out to find Lili and Diana waiting expectantly for him at the exit, which lay behind a jagged, roughly circular portion of rock which had been rolled aside.

'Now, Alan, I must leave you and return,' said Lili. 'Perhaps in the past I have at times been a little ruthless, but I beg you to remember me kindly — not to think too harshly of a poor half-caste girl who found that the ideals of the West were, after all, worthwhile! When I have gone back into the passage, roll the boulder over the mouth of the tunnel. It moves quite easily.'

'You can't go back there,' Alan protested. 'They're bound to find out what you've done, and I doubt if even your father's regard for you could save you a terrible vengeance! Come with us, Lili. You've proved yourself!'

Lili shook her head. 'I cannot. I do not fit into your world, I know it. It would break my heart to know you can never love me!'

'Then I'm afraid I must take you by force,' grunted Alan. 'You see, to go back there would mean certain death! Within a matter of a few minutes the Temple of the Purple Dragon and all its ramifications will exist no more!'

'What — what do you mean?' gasped Lili wildly.

Alan wasted no time in explanation. With one sweep of his arms he gathered the half-caste girl up and, nodding to Diana, he began to run towards the cover of a rocky embankment close by.

Safely behind this he crouched down, forcing Lili and Diana to crouch also. Tensely they waited, the girls not knowing what to expect. Then it came: the darkness of the night was split asunder by a gigantic rushing noise. Like a clap of doom, a sound like mighty thunder beat against their eardrums, and the point above the rocks in which the temple lay became a whirling fog of smoke, dust and flame. For seconds the orange glare stayed in the sky, while successive explosions rent the heavens and snapped at the teeth of the black night. The valley was illuminated by incredible lambent fires, shimmering and sparkling on the yellowness of the mimosa blooms.

Fragments of wood and stone pelted down to earth in a great cascade, and the three fugitives hid their heads behind the protective rocks.

And at last came silence; a silence deeper than that of the grave. And Lili said blankly, miserably, 'Alan — what did you do?'

Alan bit his lip. He had known that she held a very real affection for her father, and he hated to have to hurt her after what she had done for them. But he said quietly, 'I'm sorry, Lili. I had to do it! It's much better this way. Your father would have set up fresh headquarters had we escaped, and countless other people would have been killed, sacrificed. The Tong would have gone on until, someday, all would be lost, and your father would have had to bend his head before the sword of the executioner.'

'But — what did you *do*?'

'When you left along the secret passage, I went back to the storeroom. I led a long fuse from the inner chamber to an open case of dynamite. I lit it.'

'Then — they will all be — dead?'

Alan nodded his head. 'I hope so! It was swift and sure, and the Purple Dragon Tong will operate no more.'

'There is one thing I would like to do,' Lili told him. 'It may be that some of them are maimed, injured, lying there in pain and waiting for death. My father may be such a one, even. I would like you to let me have the revolvers you hold — you do not need them now — so that I may return and kill swiftly any who live and are — in pain!'

'I'm sorry, Lili. I can't trust you with a revolver. How do I know you will not turn it on us?'

'Then at least leave Diana here, and return with me to kill off those that are wounded!'

'I agree,' said Diana. 'We can't possibly leave them lying there. I will wait here, but hurry back, Alan — darling!'

Alan, gazing at Lili, saw the hurt in her eyes at this affectionate form of address. He nodded.

Together, he and Lili climbed over the rock onto the scene of dust, debris and desolation. Not a trace of the temple remained. Only smoking ruins, lumps of painted wood, jagged stone slabs. Even the seven walls were smouldering relics.

They hunted about and did indeed find one or two severely injured men, moaning in agony. These Alan mercifully shot in the brain. He turned to look for Lili, but could find no trace of her. He wandered about the wreckage, calling, but received no reply.

Where the altar and the Dragon had stood he found the wooden head of the effigy, shattered irreparably. Beside it lay a crushed and battered white man, his face mutilated beyond any hope of recognition.

Alan turned him over and noted the bald head; found, in a pocket of the

164

man's robe, a worn briar pipe. A sudden intuition told him that that briar pipe was the one used by the Reverend Harper. He experienced a shock of surprise, having not yet been told of the real identity of the Master. He shook his head and went round a pile of rubble.

Lili was there; she was standing straight and still, a long knife, which she had found, poised above her breast. Alan called, 'For God's sake, don't do *that!*'

'I must, Alan. There is no other way for me. I have betrayed my father, killed him. Your heart lies elsewhere, and I would rather be dead than see you married to another.'

'No Western-minded girl would commit suicide,' said Alan, hoping that would bring her to her senses.

Lili smiled and shook her head. 'Perhaps, after all, the ways of the East are stronger in me than I had known.'

Casting argument to the wind, Alan ran forward wildly, to endeavour to seize her hand before it could complete its work. But his foot caught against a stone; his already weak ankle twisted under him and he fell, his head smashing against a stone with sickening force.

He was only out for a second or two, but when he came round his mind had miraculously cleared. He remembered who and what he was, and how all this had come to pass. Every detail of his life up to the moment was present. He had found himself again. And, unlike so many amnesia cases, he could still recall all that had occurred while his memory had been impaired.

His eyes sought about him for Lili, and found her.

She was lying there, not two feet away. The hilt of the jewelled knife protruded from her breast, and her eyes were already glazing with the stare of death.

Sadly, he knelt on one knee beside her. Her eyes managed to register recognition, and a faint smile played over her smooth face. Her lips parted slightly, and ignoring the trickle of blood which came from them, Alan leaned forward and pressed his own to hers.

Then the smile faded from her face,

those dark, magnetic eyes closed, and Lili Lee was dead.

Whatever she had done in the past, her sins were fully atoned for. And Alan returned to Diana with a drawn face.

# 15

## The Man Who Knew Himself Again

The magnificent liner steamed into the bay, funnels belching smoke, foghorn hooting joyously.

On the deck stood a young man and a young woman. The man was tall and handsome, with wavy dark hair and a square jaw. The woman was a good match for him: slim and supple, with tawny gold hair and a dimpled smile. Her skin bore the tan of other lands. On her face was a look of wonder as the Statue of Liberty thrust upwards from the calm waters of the bay. It was her first visit to America, the first time she had ever seen the statue. She was fascinated by the gaunt, towering lines of the skyscrapers; enthralled by the city of wonder which, unable to thrust outwards and sideways, had instead expanded towards the stars, regal and forbidding. But she was more fascinated, more enthralled, by the man at her side.

She said, 'It's wonderful! I'd love to work here. Are you sure you can get me a job on your newspaper?'

'I'm positive! After the scoop I gave them about the Tong they couldn't refuse me anything — even the editor's special cigars!'

'Oh, I'm going to love it! I'll miss China, of course, but I'll be seeing plenty of you, won't I?'

'I hope so!' The young man, flushed a little, said, 'There's something I meant to ask you, but . . . well, I thought I'd give you time to forget the horror you've been through first.'

'What is it, Alan?' asked Diana softly.

'Well, now that I've got a name again, and I remember that I haven't any connections in the world, I thought I'd like to give that name to someone else — if she'll have it. Will you, Diana?'

Diana clasped his hand tightly, and said, 'Of course I will! I've been longing to hear you say that ever since we left China!'

Oblivious to the passengers, their lips

met in a long kiss.

Finally, Diana said, 'Er — Alan, did you really ever think much of poor Lili?'

'Good Lord, no!' said the man. 'Forget it! I liked the poor kid, but there was never anything else.'

Diana sighed with contentment and nestled her head against his shoulder. She didn't know it was a lie — a white lie, but still a lie.

For Alan had thought a little more of Lili than he cared for her to know; and as they came to anchor, above the New York skyline he could see the phantom outline of dark eyes; could smell the vague, subtle perfume which he recalled so well; and a voice seemed to whisper:

'Goodbye . . . Remember me, Alan!'

# Sinister Honeymoon

# Prologue

High in the Transylvanian Alps, close by a small village called Safnia, stands the mighty, grey-walled castle of the Gräfshens. In the early eighteenth century, while in England the armies of Queen Anne fought bloody battles with the French, Safnia, overshadowed by Gräfshen castle and far removed from strife and fear, lay shrouded in tenuous grey ground mists, as the evening shadows began to lengthen over the mountains.

A small party of four people trod silently, slowly, in the castle grounds, to the ancient vaults which had always been the resting place of the Counts of Gräfshen.

On their shoulders they bore a lead casket; their haunted eyes darted furtively to and fro in the thickening fog, and now and then they stole a wide-eyed glance at the casket they carried.

They reached the vault and, still

without speaking, unlocked the creaking door and trod cautiously down the cobwebbed stone steps. The leader of the party lit a candle, and the coffin was laid gingerly beside its predecessors.

The priest, for such was the leader, indicated that they should be patient. And then, in low tones, he began to murmur a prayer over the casket which bore the inscription:

'Count Elgin Gräfshen — 1635–1702.'

But his prayer was not for the dead man. It was a prayer for the living; a prayer that the Count might rest here eternally . . .

*And might never rise!*

As the monotonous words fell slowly from his lips, the candle suddenly flickered in the gloom and abruptly died out.

The bearers waited for no more: as one man they tore from that place of death, the priest well to the fore. Outside they paused, panting, while the Father locked and chained the rusty iron doors.

This done, the four commenced to retrace their steps from the castle, down into the village. No one spoke until the village gates came into view.

Then the Burgomaster of Safnia said: 'I still insist, Father, that we should have driven a stake through the accursed man's body — and buried him at the crossroads. He was evil, given to practicing the black arts — and he committed suicide! It is these things which breed vampires!'

The others crossed themselves hastily.

'My son,' said the priest gravely, 'we may not judge a man by his past — we have no right to treat him as a vampire.'

The Burgomaster was unconvinced. He continued, 'We shall see — they have all been evil, the Gräfshens. And Elgin Gräfshen — the last of them, thank God — was most evil of all.'

'What will become of the castle, now there are no others?' inquired the local innkeeper.

The priest shook his head uncertainly. 'It says in the will, Jacques, that the castle is to be closed and locked — and that thus it must remain until it falls in ruins.'

'You think it will?'

'I think so. There is a lease which does not yet expire for nine hundred years. Yes, the castle will not be occupied.'

'That was a strange clause,' whispered Jacques. 'Why did Count Elgin leave such a request in his will?'

The Burgomaster replied, after a fearful glance back at the gaunt, mist-shrouded castle towering grimly on the hill above Safnia, '*I* know. So that he may walk there; so that he may leave his coffin and prowl . . . '

'You talk the talk of a fool,' snapped the priest. 'Be quiet. Elgin Gräfshen is dead!'

'Then why did you ask God to grant that he *lay still?*'

The priest made no reply, and the innkeeper crossed himself again and said, 'Holy Mother protect us . . . '

# 1

## The Reluctant Cab-Driver

The train from Bucharest puffed leisurely into the station at Iswaldia, just as the sun dipped behind the far hills and threw the small township into the grip of an ominous darkness.

Jerry Liddon — English, bronzed, clear-eyed and fair-haired — climbed laboriously down from the compartment, burdened by some four suitcases and two hatboxes. He was followed by his pretty bride, Angela Trevor — now Angela Liddon — whose small features, tip-tilted nose and dark, glossy hair contrasted greatly with the appearance of her husband.

'Well,' exploded Jerry, 'what a journey! Why the devil did you want to be married in Bucharest, dear?'

'Oh, I don't know — just a whim, I suppose,' she replied with a smile. 'With my mother being Rumanian I've always had a fond feeling for the country — and besides, I thought that we'd be able to spend our honeymoon night in Mother's birthplace, Safnia, if we were married fairly near to it.'

'Hmm! But I understand Safnia is still about thirty miles from here?'

'That's true, but it won't take long to cover that. I've written and ordered rooms at the local inn there. Honestly, dear, I'm dying to see where Mother was born. It's something in my blood!'

Jerry grinned and said, 'You may not find it so romantic when we get there — I believe these Balkan inns have only cold running water, and that comes in by way of the roof!'

'Oh, don't be such a grump, Jerry. You don't notice little things like that on honeymoon — at least you aren't supposed to!'

Jerry glanced at her trim figure and smiled. He said, 'I don't suppose I shall, actually, darling. Well, shall we hire a taxi cab and start moving?'

She nodded eagerly, and they left the

ramshackle station and emerged into an even more ramshackle main street. There was no sign of life, apart from a peasant in a queerly shaped soft felt hat. He sported a lank moustache which effectively concealed his mouth, and an original assortment of whiskers on his cheeks. Behind all this shrubbery lurked a cunning, avaricious expression. As the travellers emerged, he doffed the hat in a sweeping salute and shuffled forward a few paces.

'Good evening, my friends,' he said in the language of the place. 'You seek a conveyance?'

'We do,' Angela told him in the same language, while Jerry strained his brains to pick up the conversation. 'Have you a car?'

The man showed his teeth in a flashing grin. 'Yes, madam, I have — at least, it is not a car, but it will carry you in comfort and with much less noise — see, yonder!' He flung out a proud arm and pointed to the roadway. Leaning up against the curb, apparently tied together with odds and ends of string, was an ancient and dilapidated carriage. Four wobbly wheels supported the closed compartment; two flimsy shafts supported the two tired-looking horses.

'Does it go?' enquired Jerry sarcastically in English.

'What does your companion say?' asked the coachman.

'Er — oh nothing, nothing,' said Angela hastily. 'We were hoping to obtain some faster conveyance than a horse-drawn vehicle,' she explained. 'Is there not a garage . . . or a motor car or bus?'

'Madam, you are in Iswaldia, not Bucharest,' pointed out the peasant disagreeably. 'This is the only means of transport. But surely time matters little? Why, I can drive you to anywhere in Iswaldia in, say, fifteen minutes.'

'But we aren't staying in Iswaldia; we still have thirty miles to go. How long would that take you?'

The peasant considered. He counted reflectively on his fingers, then glanced towards his toes, as if seeking further mathematical aids. In this he was foiled by the intervention of his stout boots. Finally he said: 'I could accomplish thirty miles in — provided there are no breakdowns — about three hours ... possibly,' he added cautiously.

'What does he say?' demanded Jerry.

'Says it would take him three hours — perhaps,' Angela sighed. 'Well, we'll have to take his offer, Jerry — there isn't any other way, I'm afraid.'

Jerry groaned, and Angela smiled and kissed him quickly. 'I know it's an awful lot of trouble, dear, but I promise you I'll make it up to you tonight.'

At which the suffering bridegroom brightened up noticeably and slung the luggage aboard the carriage, which creaked a stern warning against the sudden weight. They mounted, and the driver climbed to his seat. 'Where is your destination?' he asked.

'The inn at Safnia,' Angela told him.

For a moment there was a stunned silence. Then the driver dismounted again and peered through the door at them. 'You-you are going to-to Safnia?' he gasped.

'But of course. Why shouldn't we be going to Safnia?'

'But it is so beautiful here, in Iswaldia!

181

Why go to Safnia? You will not like it there, I tell you. It is such a miserable place it would make you sick to look at it! Now here in Iswaldia, we have the finest hotel in the country . . . Permit that I should drive you there, where you will be made very welcome!' He gazed at them hopefully.

'We,' said Angela coldly, 'do not wish to stay in Iswaldia. We wish to go to Safnia. Do you mind?'

'But the hotel here is the finest — '

'We do not doubt the quality of your hotel,' snapped Angela, rattled. 'Nor do we doubt the beauty at Iswaldia — although we can see little enough of it at the moment. Nevertheless, we wish to go to Safnia — and, in fact, we are going to Safnia.'

'Then, madam, I regret, not in my carriage.'

'What?'

The driver shook his head with finality. 'I cannot drive you to Safnia — unless you will wait until morning,' he explained. 'To reach Safnia, one must pass the castle of the Counts of Gräfshen . . . '

'What has that to do with it?'

'Nothing — if one manages to pass it! But often one does not! There have been tales told . . . tales of wayfarers who have ventured too near the castle at night and, in the morning, have been found with . . . *ugh*!' He shuddered and crossed himself.

Jerry cut in, 'When you've finished your little cross talk act, Angela, will you let me know what's holding up the troops?'

Angela shrugged angrily. 'He refuses to drive us to Safnia through the night,' she snapped, 'because we must pass Gräfshen Castle! He is afraid.'

'Good Lord! Afraid of what?'

'The fool is afraid of — vampires!' said Angela.

The cigarette Jerry was holding snapped suddenly under the involuntary pressure of his fingers. He gasped, '*What*?'

'Vampires, dear. You know, the things which are supposed to suck the blood from the living. They leave their graves every night, and . . . of course, it's a lot of nonsense. My mother used to tell me about the Gräfshen vampires, but I put it all down to the silly superstitions she learned when she was a child. Which of course, it was! There isn't any room for vampires in the twentieth century; *you* know that, dear.'

'Ye gods,' moaned Jerry, 'why didn't you mention this before?'

'I didn't think it was worth mentioning. Naturally you don't believe in such rot.'

'Naturally. But it seems these fellows do, and that's going to hold us up, by the look of things. Show him some money and see if that talks. It usually has something to say.'

Angela extracted her purse and flourished money before the driver. His eyes gleamed, but he still shook his head.

'Useless,' said Angela. 'If that won't persuade him, nothing will. We'll just have to put up here for tonight and get on our way in the morning.'

Jerry was actually reaching for his luggage when from the shelter of the station stepped a tall, thin aristocratic man. His clothes were quiet but fashionable, and he could have been recognized as English anywhere. He stepped across to the carriage, peered at its occupants and said, 'Is this your carriage?'

'It was,' Jerry agreed. 'We were going to Safnia.'

'Safnia? Excellent! Then I trust you will permit me to share it with you?'

Jerry shook his head. 'I'm sorry — you're welcome as far as I'm concerned, but the driver doesn't seem to relish the idea of going to Safnia, so I'm afraid that takes the matter out of my hands.'

The thin man turned to the driver and spoke to him in fluent vernacular. 'You refuse to drive to Safnia? May I ask why?'

The driver spread his hands regretfully. 'Vampires . . . '

'Vampires? Vampires! You dolt, are you afraid of a silly superstition? Vampires, indeed! Look here, my man — you've got this carriage out here for hire, and that being the case, it is illegal for you to refuse a fare. You understand?'

The driver nodded, though he didn't understand. He wasn't sure if the Englishman was talking through his hat, but he didn't like to argue — the thin man had that compelling air.

'Good! Then do you prefer to spend a night in the local police station, or to drive us to Safnia?'

As if in a daze, the driver mounted again. He said, 'I'll drive you as far as Baria Hill . . . then you must walk!'

# 2

## Strange Encounter

As the coach rattled out of the village along a curved upward trail, through thick belts of trees, the thin stranger settled himself on the seat opposite the Liddons and smiled at them.

'Perhaps I should introduce myself,' he said amiably. 'If we are to be companions in a confined space for the next three hours or so, I think that would ease the embarrassment, would it not?'

Jerry said, 'This is my wife, Angela Liddon. I am Jerry Liddon. Thanks for handling the driver so nicely. We were afraid we should have to cancel our journey for the night.'

'That's quite all right. I am as anxious as you appear to be to reach Safnia at once. I am Henry Hartnell. Possibly you have heard of me — or am I unduly conceited?'

'Why, no, Mister Hartnell,' exclaimed Angela. 'We've heard of you — haven't we, Jerry?'

'We certainly have — and it's a pleasure to make your acquaintance, sir. We have an entire shelf filled with your books at our new home. *Legends of Werewolves, The Black Arts, The Devil and His Disciples*, and many more.'

'You enjoyed them, I hope?' said the other with a smile.

Jerry flushed. 'Well, to be frank, I'm afraid we haven't read them yet. You see, they were a gift from a friend of ours — a wedding gift — and we are only just married.'

'I see. Congratulations. But I must warn you that they are not sincere works — not by any means. I myself do not believe in ghosts, apparitions, demons, witchcraft, werewolves, or vampires.'

'And yet you are a noted writer on those subjects? Not decrying them, but encouraging people to believe there really is something behind old tales and legends . . . '

'I really shouldn't be telling you this, I

suppose, but at least it helps to break the ice. My books are all written with tongue in cheek. I found there was a market for works of that nature, and I simply turned my hand to writing what the public wished to read. That's all. As for believing what I write myself, well, I'm not quite that simple, Mister Liddon.'

'I see. I suppose quite a lot of books are written in that way — I mean, without their authors believing in the things they write.'

'That is so. A writer must have the ability to lose himself in his subject — to write what his readers wish to read, and not what he knows to be the truth. Those who adhere to principles hardly ever succeed, Mister Liddon.'

'I suppose you are up here looking for material? Or are you merely vacationing?' asked Angela with a smile.

'You were right first time, Mrs. Liddon. I am here to work. Gathering material for my next book, as a matter of fact. It is to deal with vampirism, of course. That is why I felt the finest place to gain colour would be Safnia. As you know, up here in these old hills, the people are all extremely childlike in their beliefs — I might almost say moronic. And the legend of the Gräfshen Vampire persists strongly to this day. I hope to gather sufficient material to cover at least twenty thousand words.'

'I am sure you will,' Angela told him. 'My mother used to tell me quite a lot about the Vampire of Gräfshen. Of course, I have no more belief than yourself in the stories. It is utterly ridiculous to suppose that any person could exist after death by drinking the blood from a sleeping person's throat.'

The conversation died soon after that, and the three passengers stared curiously from the windows at the ghosts of tall trees which loomed eerily through the thickening mists. From nearby marshes they could hear the harsh croaking of the bullfrogs and the weird, flutelike call of a night bird.

Hartnell penciled scrawly notes in a notebook, and in the dimness of the coach Jerry slipped his arm about Angela's slender form and drew her close to him. They rattled on for hours, and Hartnell fell into sleep, his notebook falling from his relaxed fingers.

Upwards, ever upwards they went, into the heart of the mountain country. Once or twice they passed a village, hardly visible through the murk, but finally even these stray signs of civilization had gone, and Safnia drew steadily nearer.

They breasted the top of a steep rise, and here the coachman pulled up and slid from his seat. He opened the door and awakened the three travellers, who were now all asleep.

'Here's Baria Hill,' he told them in a surly tone. 'This is where you get off and walk. If you'd listened to me, you'd have stayed at Iswaldia for the night. The hotel there is — '

'Yes, yes, yes,' said Hartnell testily. 'What do we owe you, my man?'

The driver named an exorbitant price, but Hartnell paid it without quibbling. Jerry protested, and Hartnell smiled and waved his protestations aside. 'No, no, Liddon. I insist. You must allow me to foot this bill. And now,' he said, turning to the driver, 'exactly how do we reach Safnia?'

The driver licked his lips and peered furtively about. Then he led them over the rise and pointed into the thick blanket of mist beyond. 'See that deeper patch in the mist?' he asked. Hartnell nodded. 'That's Gräfshen Castle. You'll have to go past that by the coach trail. Immediately below it, about twenty minutes' walk, you will find Safnia. Keep to the trail, for the drops on either side of the cliff are very dangerous. It will be awkward in this mist, but you will manage, I think. That is, if nothing happens . . . '

'Pah!' snorted the writer. 'On your way, man! Take your bogies with you!'

The man grunted and swung back to his seat. With a flick of the wrist he turned his moth-eaten nags and swung off down the trail back to Iswaldia and its wonderful hotel.

The stranded travellers gazed at each other helplessly. Jerry dumped his cases down and said, 'Well, this is a fine mess! We're faced by sheer falls into precipitous chasms, and prowling vampires! What a honeymoon!'

'Cheer up,' said Hartnell. 'It isn't that bad. I think we can afford to ignore the vampires; the cliffs are all we have to worry about. My eyes are pretty poor — too much writing; perhaps you could lead the way?'

'I will,' volunteered Angela. 'Jerry's loaded down with luggage, and my eyes are pretty good. We'll struggle through if it takes all night!'

'What a honeymoon,' groaned Jerry again, as the party started dolefully in the direction of the castle trail.

Sliding and stumbling down the hilly pathway, they drew nearer to the gates of Gräfshen Castle. Angela, being in the lead, was first to see the car which lay with its nose against a tree on the path side. She halted and turned to her companions. 'It's a car — a modern car, up here in the Transylvanian hills! What on earth . . . '

'Looks as if someone came a nasty smack against that tree,' said Jerry, scrutinizing the car bonnet. 'Probably finished the engine off, and had to walk the rest of the way to Safnia.'

Hartnell tried the car doors and found them locked. He shrugged and said, 'Let's get on — we'll find out about the car when we get to the village.'

They started again, Angela leading. The mist had lifted slightly, and from above, the pale spectre of a moon was striving to shed its rays upon the castle. Now they could see the gaunt turrets and battlements, where bats and owls flitted silently to and fro, and damp green moss curtained the wet and decaying woodwork of the doors.

A long, sobbing scream of terror echoed dully through the night.

'*What . . . ?*'

They halted abruptly, Angela going pale. Jerry dropped his cases and placed an arm about her waist to calm her shudders.

Then it came again — that cry of hideous fear. Muffled by the mist, it rose, then died away again into a barely audible moan. Then it came no more.

'It sounded like a woman,' breathed Hartnell, peering hard through the gloom. 'It came from down there — in the direction of the castle!'

'Perhaps — perhaps someone has fallen over the cliff?' suggested Jerry.

'I think not — no, in that case there would have been only the one scream, and it would not have lasted so long. I think we had better get down there as rapidly as possible and investigate. Follow me . . . '

With Jerry beside him and Angela hanging onto her husband's arm, they trotted rapidly towards the castle.

The gates loomed up unexpectedly, and Hartnell, without pause, pushed them open and entered the grounds. The squeal of rusty hinges had hardly died away before Hartnell cried, 'My God! What's that?'

The three travellers stood frozen to the spot. Their eyes strained towards a patch of ground in front of them — towards the dark, cloaked figure which was bending over the form of a woman in a white dress, who lay upon the damp earth. Bending over her, its face low above her neck!

Jerry roared, 'You damned prowler — '

The black-garbed figure rose slowly

and confronted them, its pallid, death-mask face expressionless in the white mist. From above a cruel hooked nose, two eyes like burning coals stared in their direction. Red-hued lips parted, and the figure said, 'I beg your pardon . . . I fear this young lady has met with an accident.' The voice was a soft, throaty blubber, as if it forced its way past a mouth congested with blood!

Jerry stepped grimly forward, Hartnell on his heels.

'I found her wandering in the grounds,' explained the dark prowler. 'When she saw me I fear she received a severe shock. I was about to see if I could do anything for her, when she screamed and, apparently, fainted . . . '

Jerry knelt by the girl and almost gasped. The white dress she wore beneath the heavy motoring coat, which now lay open, outlined her voluptuous feline figure to full advantage. Her eyes were closed, but her red hair framed a face which would have done credit to a Follies beauty: full, smooth lips; dainty nose; wide, clear brow; and a soft, rounded chin over a white column of throat, about which were looped a double string of pearls. Her hands were tightly clenched by her side, and a trickle of blood ran from a cut on her forehead.

'She's dead out,' said Jerry. 'I suppose this is the girl who owns the car back there? Possibly she cut her head when she hit that tree.'

Hartnell nodded. Angela said nothing, but remained staring at the white-faced man who, beneath his cape, was attired in sober black evening dress.

'I don't think we have had the pleasure,' said the man, a smile curving his lips and sunken cheeks. 'My name is Count Elgin Gräfshen.'

'I'm Hartnell — Henry Hartnell. My friends here are Mr. and Mrs. Liddon.'

'I think we'd better get the girl down to the village,' said Jerry. 'This cut needs attention.'

'Perhaps the Count can supply us with the means of doctoring the wound?' Hartnell suggested.

Count Gräfshen spread his hands regretfully. 'No, I am sorry. The castle has been closed a long time. I do not use it, you see. I am afraid there would be nothing there. It would, perhaps, be best if you left the girl in my care and went on to the village for medical supplies.'

Jerry looked him in the eyes and disliked what he saw. 'Thank you, Count, but I think we'll take her along. Mr. Hartnell and I can manage.' He wrapped a clean handkerchief about the girl's head, and he and Hartnell together lifted her from the ground.

The Count followed them to the gates, opened them, and watched the party move into the road. 'Be careful,' he said softly. 'There are dangerous drops about here. And perhaps when the young lady is recovered, you would honour me with a further visit?'

'Possibly we will, Count,' Hartnell assured him.

They commenced to move down the trail. Angela turned to look once more at the sinister figure of Count Elgin — and a disbelieving cry tore from her lips.

The Count had gone! Vanished, seemingly into thin air!

'Jerry,' she panted. 'The-the Count — he's-he's gone!'

'What of it? No sense in him hanging round, is there?'

'No, but — he — seemed to just — vanish. Oh, I know you will think I'm silly, but Jerry, I — I think . . . '

'Go on. You think what?'

'I think — he's a — vampire!'

'In heaven's name, why? He was a queer-looking bird, I admit, but why should he be a vampire? I thought you didn't believe in things like that?'

'I didn't — but his name! Count Elgin Gräfshen! And my mother told me that Count Elgin, last of the Gräfshens, hung himself in the castle in 1702!'

From the grounds they had just left floated a soft, obscene chuckle.

# 3

## Mark of the Vampire?

They had almost reached the gates of the village when the senseless girl opened her eyes and looked round her dazedly. She opened her mouth to cry out, but Jerry gripped her arm and said, 'Easy now — you're all right. We're taking you down to the village.'

'Safnia?' she said in low, deep tones.

'Safnia. That's it. What happened to you?'

Her brow wrinkled as she strove to make her memory function again. She said slowly, uncertainly, 'I was in my car, heading for Safnia. The car stopped when I hit a tree trunk by the side of the path, and — I couldn't start it again. I got out and started to walk . . . I hadn't any idea how far away the village was, and when I saw a castle I decided to try and contact someone . . .

'I couldn't have walked much further . . . My head was cut in the car crash, and was bleeding badly. I'd just got inside the castle gates when I saw a dark figure with awful eyes coming towards me in the darkness. Those eyes were terrible — they frightened me out of my wits, and I screamed . . . I guess I must have passed out — '

'You're quite all right now,' said Hartnell with a smile. 'You must have mistaken the Count for a ghost or something.'

'She wasn't so far wrong — ' began Angela, but Jerry hastily cut in.

'What were you doing up here in this mist in a car, Miss . . . ?'

'Storm,' she told him. 'I'm Gail Storm. Perhaps you've seen me before . . . '

'We seem to be snowed under with celebrities today,' said Jerry. 'We've seen you often, Miss Storm. It's a wonder we didn't recognize you! You make cinema films for Excelda Studios in Hollywood, don't you?'

'I'm flattered. Yes, I admit the charge. We were up here on location for a picture, and when the rest went home I liked the country so much I decided to hang on a couple of weeks and tour around by car. I had only meant to pass through Safnia and stay one night, but it looks as if I shall be stuck there now until this wound heals.'

'That shouldn't be long, Miss Storm,' Hartnell told her. 'My name is Henry Hartnell, and your other bearer is Jerry Liddon. The young lady is his wife, Angela.'

Gail Storm glanced curiously at Angela, then at Jerry. Then she smiled, her eyes closed, and she appeared to go into a sleep.

In a matter of minutes they had reached the village gates. They were tightly locked, and Hartnell cursed softly and began to hammer on them. For some time there was no reply, but soon they heard the clatter of boots on cobblestones, and a quavering voice demanded to know who was without.

'Open up!' shouted Hartnell. 'Is this a sample of your Sylvanian hospitality?'

'Who are you that come so late to Safnia?' called the voice tremblingly.

'We aren't vampires,' shouted back Jerry, and he heard the quick intake of breath from the other side. 'Hurry up and open this gate. We have an injured woman here who badly needs medical aid.'

'Injured? Woman? How — how injured?'

'Head injuries,' replied Hartnell.

'Not — not — throat injuries?'

'No!'

Cautiously the gate was unchained and swung open. The man in charge peered through at them, and apparently satisfied as to their authenticity, permitted them to enter. 'I am sorry I caused you to wait,' he mumbled. 'But evil forces have been strong here lately. Since last Walpurgis Nacht they have given us no rest!'

'Tripe,' said Hartnell in English. Then, in the vernacular: 'Where can we find the inn?'

Carefully the man locked the gate again, then gestured towards a small wooden building set on the right-hand side of a nearby square. 'You will have to awaken Franz, the innkeeper,' he explained. 'And he is a very heavy sleeper.'

The travellers nodded and moved

through the silent streets to the main square and the inn front. Here, upon a strong bolt-studded door, Hartnell beat a tattoo with his shoe heel. After a few seconds of this, a second-floor window shot up and a gross night-capped head protruded; beneath it was a face white and terrified. 'What is it, what is it? He — he has been abroad again?' The man's voice was filled with fear, and Hartnell hastened to reassure him.

'We are travellers seeking shelter,' he called. 'There are four of us — three of us who have ordered rooms, and an injured lady. Kindly admit us immediately!'

'Fine time of night to arrive,' grumbled the head, withdrawing suddenly in disgust.

Within a few minutes the door opened and they entered the inn. It was an old-world place, heavy with oaken beams and great fireplaces. Angela, but for the circumstances, would have found it quite up to her expectations.

The weary travellers settled before the immense log fire, and the landlord put on more fuel until it roared into the wide chimney. He brought along bandages and lint, and while Hartnell bandaged Gail Storm's head, Jerry and Angela revived themselves with hot drinks which the landlord thoughtfully provided. Sandwiches were served and the party, including Franz the innkeeper, settled round the fire to warm up before going to their rooms.

'From where have you come tonight?' he queried of them.

'From Iswaldia, three of us. The other young lady was in her car.'

'I came from Slatina,' she told them.

'By car?' enquired the innkeeper. 'Then what have you done with your conveyance?'

'I had an accident — hit a tree trunk. I had to leave it up the hill and walk down here.'

'What?' The innkeeper's eyes were almost popping from his grotesque skull. 'You — you walked past Gräfshen Castle? Were you alone?'

'Why, yes. These other people didn't join me until later.'

'Did — did you — see anything?' The

fear in Franz's voice was patent, and when Gail told him of her encounter with Count Elgin Gräfshen, his grip tightened convulsively upon the wooden arms of his chair.

'Count Elgin Gräfshen?' he stammered. 'Did he — did he harm — you?'

'Good heavens, no; why should he?'

'He was quite charming,' said Hartnell. 'We came up just as he was bending over Miss Storm to aid her.'

'Bending over her — Count Elgin?' whispered the man.

'Yes — you see, she was unconscious when we reached her. She got a fright through coming upon the Count suddenly.'

'But — don't you understand, you fools?' said the innkeeper vehemently. 'Count Elgin Gräfshen is a vampire! The entire village is afraid of him. No one ventures out after darkness has fallen, and we keep the gates tightly locked.'

'Mrs. Liddon also thinks the Count is a vampire,' agreed the writer. 'But really, sir, you can't expect rational men to believe such a tale!'

'No?' The innkeeper suddenly moved forward, until he was standing above Gail Storm. His right hand whipped out and she shrank back in surprise as the double-link of pearls were whipped from her neck.

'How dare you!' cried Hartnell angrily.

'Look!' breathed the innkeeper, and Hartnell's anger faded as his eyes turned towards the girl's white throat. Immediately above the jugular vein were two small marks in the flesh — red, blood-smeared marks. The throat about them was red as if it had been recently drawn by suction . . .

'The mark of the vampire!' hissed Franz, his face paler than ever.

Momentarily stunned by the implication of those two marks, the party were motionless, silent, unable to think of anything to say or do. It was a tableau cut from stone: the girl film star, shrinking away on the low settee, and her companions staring at her neck with horrified eyes.

Then the tension snapped. Hartnell snapped it, as neatly as if he had severed a piece of string with a sharp knife. He said, 'Nonsense! Because Miss Storm has two marks on her throat, it certainly doesn't say they've been made by a vampire! Possibly she has some explanation which would account for their presence?'

Gail Storm was breathing more quickly, her fingers fumbling in her handbag. They emerged gripping a small mirror, the knuckles white with the tautness of her grasp. She raised it slowly, fearfully to her neck and stared at the two tiny marks there — marks which might easily have been made by sharp, pointed teeth. They watched her as she looked; saw her struggle to control something, some mental stress. Then she said, 'Why — why yes . . . They — they are easily explained. I — I had a brooch — a present it was — and until recently I have been wearing it. I discarded it because of the marks it left.'

'Do you, then, wear a brooch so high up on your throat?' said Franz.

'Er — as a rule, no. But I was wearing it with a high-necked blouse.' She glanced appealingly towards Hartnell, and he rushed to her rescue.

'That satisfactorily settles that,' he exclaimed easily. 'And now, if you will be good enough to show us to our rooms?'

Franz shook his head. 'I am not satisfied! I still think this woman has been bitten by Count Elgin — and such being the case, it is unsafe for her to stay here.'

'Nonsense. What harm can come to her here?'

'No harm can come to her — none! But her presence in my inn will endanger us all! She must leave, at once!'

Hartnell rose to his feet. His eyes were dangerous as he faced the fat innkeeper. He snapped, 'The lady has said those marks were caused by a brooch. Are you venturing to call her a liar, my man?'

The innkeeper shrank visibly. He whispered, 'No, no. You mistake me. But I can afford to take no chances. My daughter, Netta . . . my wife . . . I dare not risk exposing them to any danger — '

'What danger can there be here?'

'The bite,' explained Franz, shuddering. 'Have you not heard it? You write of these things. You must know.'

'I think I do know what you refer to

. . . and I warn you that I will not have Miss Storm further upset by your stupid superstitions. I forbid you to mention it, do you hear?'

Jerry could not help admiring the impressive figure the author made, standing there, his eyes flashing at the fat landlord. And his air of command, of accustomed ease to being obeyed, cowed Franz. He murmured: 'If you wish it so, sir.'

'And now,' said Hartnell, 'I would be obliged if you would show Miss Storm and myself to our rooms. I feel exceptionally tired after the journey, and I am sure Miss Storm feels so, too.' He glanced at Gail Storm in a way which clearly told everyone present he was more than mildly, or courteously, interested in that young lady.

She smiled at him, and with one hand to her throat to hide those marks, said, 'I do feel rather tired, Mr. Hartnell.'

Muttering, Franz led them up the gloomy staircase.

Left alone, Jerry and Angela relaxed, and Jerry's arm stole about her waist.

'Tired, dear?' she asked, kissing his forehead.

'Tired as hell,' he agreed. 'What a honeymoon this turned out to be. I'm so tired all I want to do is sleep.'

'Me, too. But at least we're here now — and there's always tomorrow!'

'I suppose there is at that,' Jerry agreed with a smile. 'There are a whole lot of tomorrows for us, honey.'

'Did you think Gail Storm was very beautiful?' asked Angela suddenly.

'Hello,' Jerry said, grinning. 'What's this? The old green-eyed monster?'

'Why, no; I just wondered. I can't see very much in her. I mean — well, she looks — well, common. I can't honestly see why men seem to think she's — glamorous.'

'Don't worry,' Jerry said, still grinning. 'She looks as if she'll be kept fully occupied by Hartnell while he's here. And even if she wasn't, I've got all the women I can handle!' And he gave Angela a gentle squeeze.

Still muttering to himself, Franz reappeared. He saw the honeymooners together and leered at them. He said, 'Perhaps you would like to go to your rooms?'

'We would — we are rather sleepy!'

'Sleepy?' Franz stared, then rubbed his head. 'They are mad, these English,' he said to no one in particular. He led them upstairs, along a dark corridor to a room door.

Before they went in, Jerry said: 'By the way, what were you referring to before? When Hartnell stopped you?'

'It is said,' whispered the innkeeper, 'that whosoever is bitten by a vampire, *becomes themselves a vampire!*'

# 4

## The Blank Mirror

The wintry sun was streaming in through the old-fashioned casements when Jerry woke the next morning. He glanced at Angela, her tousled head beside him on the pillow, and smiled. She was still fast asleep, one small hand clutching his shoulder, as if seeking a feeling of security.

He rose, washed and dressed without waking her, and before he went down to see what happened about breakfast there, gave her a shake. Leaving her to wash in the washbowl (which was the only article for ablutions the hotel possessed), he went breezily down the stairs and into the old oak-raftered room.

Hartnell was already seated at a long wooden table, doing justice to an English breakfast of bacon and eggs, and Jerry joined him.

'I must say the food is excellent here,' Hartnell said with a smile when they had exchanged greetings. 'If nothing else is up to standard, I think I could stand a few vampires for the sake of the cooking.'

'That's the trouble with vampires,' Jerry said. 'No wonder they're a morbid type — look at their diet! Now if they were to get on the right side of a large-sized portion of bacon and eggs, or surround a plate of roast beef, I rather think they wouldn't need to trot about seeking human victims.'

'How right you are,' Hartnell agreed.

'Perhaps you could put me right on a point about vampires,' Jerry said thoughtfully. 'At least, I mean about the legends surrounding them. It's this: Is it part of the story that if a person is bitten by a vampire, they themselves become one? I know this is supposed to be so in the case of werewolf legends, but I hadn't heard it also applied to vampirism.'

'It all depends,' said Hartnell, frowning. 'Has Franz been talking to you?'

'As a matter of fact, yes.'

'Then I shouldn't mention it in front of

Miss Storm. There isn't any truth in it, of course, but it may upset her — she is a very highly strung young lady.'

'Don't worry; I wouldn't dream of saying anything which might unstring her nerves.'

'Well, these vampire legends vary with the district and country. And also with the particular vampire concerned. It isn't commonly supposed that a vampire's victim must also become a vampire — but certain villages believe this to be the case. Safnia happens to be one of them. They are very strong in their beliefs; they do not doubt the existence of this two-hundred-and-odd-year-old monster of theirs. That is why they built the wall about the village, so that it could be locked at sunset. Ridiculous, of course, but you know these ignorant peasants.'

'That's another strange point. The innkeeper! He seems to be quite a knowledgeable sort of chap, apart from his fear of anything vampirism.'

'A fixation,' explained Hartnell. 'Fear of vampires was driven into his mind since he was a mere babe in arms. No matter how his education progresses, no matter who decries his supernatural beliefs, he will continue to believe until his dying day.'

'But surely a man of even elementary intelligence could not believe in things like that? Surely he could see that in the modern twentieth-century world of bustle and machinery, vampires are out of place? That they just don't fit in?'

'He can see they don't fit in in, say, London, Paris or New York. Or any modern city, for that matter, even Bucharest. But up here, time stands still. This village, I would like to bet, has not changed one iota since they buried Count Gräfshen back in the eighteenth century. And up here, to these people, vampires have a very definite place in the scheme of life. Even today, in the civilized world, I have met men who really believe in vampirism — yes, I repeat it, Mr. Liddon. Eminent men — college professors, city business magnates, my own contemporaries.'

'I find it hard to understand that anyone with the brain of an average adult could credit these ridiculous legends. As a form of fiction, yes. But not as fact!'

'I wonder, with all our sophisticated scepticism, if we are quite right in dismissing the matter so lightly? I recall the old adage, Mr. Liddon, which says where there's smoke, there's fire. Vampires are an almost universal legend . . . '

'For heaven's sake, don't say you are beginning to place some faith in the stories?'

'After last night, Mr. Liddon, I don't know! However, I mean to accept Count Elgin's invitation tonight and go up to the castle. If he is some trickster playing a foolish practical joke, I will find him out. If not . . . who knows? Perhaps, since you are interested yourself, you would care to accompany me?'

He broke off abruptly as Gail Storm entered the room and joined them at the table. Angela came down shortly after, and Jerry received no further chance to accept Hartnell's invitation. The four travellers spent the day together and by common consent they decided to retrace the ground of their previous night's adventure. They did so.

Both the men noticed that although their own footprints and those of the two women were clearly visible in the marshy ground, those which should have been left by the Count were non-existent. However, they kept this information to themselves, not wishing to alarm the ladies.

Shortly after sunset Hartnell appeared in his overcoat, holding a heavy torch in his hand. Jerry and Angela rose as he appeared, and Jerry said, 'Are you going now, Mr. Hartnell?'

'I am. I take it you are not accompanying me?'

Jerry shook his head regretfully. 'I'm sorry, no. I'd like to — '

'I've asked him not to,' put in Angela quickly. 'If you two think the Count isn't anything abnormal, I'm convinced he is! And I don't wish to find myself a widow just yet.'

'I think you are very wise, Mrs. Liddon. However, being unmarried, I need not be so careful as your husband.'

Jerry thought he could detect a faint

sneer behind the words, but Angela's grip on his arm prevented him from speaking. She said, 'How will you know whether or not the Count is a vampire, even if you see him?'

'That's quite elementary. I thought everyone would have known the test.'

'You mean a mirror?'

'Exactly. Legend has it that vampires cast no reflection. I see no reason why our particular specimen should be an exception to that rule.'

'And your protection? A cross?'

Hartnell smiled. 'I'm afraid not, Mrs. Liddon. Of what use would a cross be to a rank atheist? No, for my protection I rely on something much more reassuring — a Colt automatic!' He paused at the door and made a slight bow to her. 'I must say that I do not anticipate having to use it! Good evening.' The door closed behind him.

Franz came hurrying in, his eyes peering questioningly here and there. He said, 'Did I hear someone leave the inn?'

'You did,' said Angela, nodding. 'Mr. Hartnell left.'

'Is it his intention to go far?'

'As far as the castle, I understand,' Jerry said. 'He's going to one of the Count's 'at-homes'!'

Franz's eyeballs swivelled wildly in their sockets. 'What, what? Holy Mother of God! The man must be insane! He will never return — never!'

'I rather think he will,' Jerry said lightly. 'Unless he happens to fall over the cliff.'

'That is nothing — there are worse perils than that about Gräfshen Castle! However, it is on his own head. The gates are locked at sundown and they will not be reopened until sunrise. I have only one regret — that he did not pay his bill before he went. Now I shall never get it!' And still mumbling, he vanished towards the kitchen.

Meanwhile, in the dying rays of the sun which still shone faintly from behind the hill, Hartnell pushed on towards the castle. He heard the village gates swing shut behind him and he was aware of the popping eyes which followed his progress up the hill.

As he neared the gates of the castle his

spirits began to ebb. Up here it was incredibly lonely, and although he could see the village and the spiralling jets of smoke from the chimneys, he might have been in another world as far as sound was concerned. Not even the croak of a bull-frog or the twitter of a bird broke the ghastly stillness about the castle itself.

Hartnell shrugged and threw off his suddenly developing fears. Humming to himself, he pushed open the old gate and stepped through into the grounds.

It struck him immediately, that sensation of something evil: a feeling that he was walking towards something unclean, unwholesome; something which had no right to exist in a world of sunshine.

He paused irresolutely, then laughed to himself and walked towards the castle, through the belt of trees. It was as it had been earlier — only now it seemed more menacing. The slitted windows were hollow eyes which peered from the grey, drab façade — peered for victims. The massive bolt-studded doors were a closed maw which would gape open when the victim appeared, and swallow him, never to disgorge him again.

Hartnell dismissed his fanciful imaginings; he always thought melodramatically. He had to, or his books would never have enjoyed their record sales.

He hammered violently on the door and waited. There was no response. He gave the door a miss, wandered round to the rear of the castle, where they had not ventured last night.

Here he saw the Tomb of the Gräfshens. If it could have been called a tomb. To Hartnell's eyes it looked more like a mausoleum. It was tall, rising from the ground in which it stood, unrelieved by a solitary window. It was built uncomfortably close to the castle itself. Hartnell wondered if there could be a reason for that.

Six steps, sunken into the ground, led down to a door below ground level. Hartnell descended them and inspected the door. It was of solid iron, long rusted over, and was secured by two immense bolts and a chain and padlock. Hartnell examined the lock and found it had not been tampered with. He struck the door a resounding blow with a piece of rock and heard the dull reverberation inside the tomb.

Again he struck at the vault door, more heavily. Then, realizing what a damned fool he must look, he cast the stone aside and glanced towards the darkening sky. The castle and grounds were covered now in half-shadows, and they shifted eerily about as he turned and remounted the steps. He took his torch from his pocket and shone it back again on the front of the vault.

'You find the resting place of my ancestors interesting?'

Hartnell spun round, a gasp escaping him in spite of himself. The Count was there, just behind him, still attired in black cape, with old-fashioned evening dress beneath it. His burning eyes bored into the writer; his thin red lips curled back from fang-like teeth; his face, dull with the fish-like pallor of death and decay, was smiling. There emanated from him a musty smell — a smell as of damp earth and mouldering shrouds.

Hartnell took a grip of himself and

said: 'Good evening, Count! I thought you had forgotten our appointment?'

'Appointment? Oh, you refer to my pressing invitation to call on me again? But I had thought you would not be quite so impetuous in accepting it. However, now you are here, perhaps I could offer you a little wine? There is very fine wine in the — cellars — here. Two hundred years old, and over. If you wish to join me . . . ?'

For a second a cold, unreasoning fear took possession of Henry Hartnell. He was convinced now that this ghoul before him was no normal human being. But he thought of the material which the encounter would afford him for his book: wine with a vampire!

He nodded. 'I should be delighted. But, may I add that I have in my pocket a revolver — a revolver which I will not hesitate to make full use of, if the occasion arises. You understand me, Count Elgin?'

The Count smiled. 'If you mean that as a warning to me, I assure you it is entirely unnecessary. No harm will come to you here. I suppose they have been filling you with their silly beliefs in the village?'

Hartnell made no reply, and the Count turned and led the way to a small door at the rear of the castle. He opened this with a touch and said, 'It is much more convenient this way. So troublesome to use the front entrance. Step inside . . . '

'I thought you didn't live at the castle?'

'I don't. I still use it, however.'

As he entered, Hartnell eased the hand mirror from his pocket and focused it upon Count Elgin's back. And with a tremor of fear he realized that it remained blank — Count Elgin Gräfshen, in the best tradition of vampires, cast no reflection!

# 5

## Hartnell's Fate

Jerry laid aside his magazine, looked over at Angela and said simply, 'Bed?'

She blushed a little, but nodded her head. She came across and sat on the arm of the chair he was in, twining her fingers through his hair, smiling down at him.

'This is our *real* honeymoon night,' she said shyly. 'I'll go up now, Jerry darling — give me a few minutes . . .'

'Sure, honey, sure. I'll follow you in about quarter of an hour.'

She smiled, kissed him on the lips and ran up the stairs. She glanced back at the top step and blew him a kiss. Franz, in the corner, gave a gloating chuckle.

Then Angela was gone, and Jerry picked up the magazine to conceal his embarrassment, and embarked upon the difficult task of reading it upside-down. After a few minutes he laid it aside, groped at his collar, fumbled with his cigarette case, spilled half the cigarettes out and nervously lit one.

'Do not worry,' Franz leered. 'It will be beautiful — ah! I remember well my own honeymoon.' He broke off to kiss his finger tips with a loud smacking noise. 'It was Paris — Paris, in the spring! A wonderful experience, with my little Elsa . . . '

At that moment his little Elsa (now fifteen stone of wobbly flesh, with a figure like an hourglass run to seed) made her entrance from the kitchens. 'Franz,' she nagged, her voice cutting like a whip, 'must you always sit lazily upon your large behind? Will you never wash the dishes without being asked continually?'

'I was just recalling our honeymoon — Paris, in the spring. Remember, my love?' said Franz in a conciliatory tone.

'Pah! Bah! How you have changed since then . . . '

'And you, my love,' said Franz slyly.

'Ha no wonder, the way I work and slave for you, you fat lazy hulk! Quickly, the dishes!'

'Coming, coming,' said Franz help-lessly. He turned to Jerry, spreading his arms wide in despair. 'You see. It is always thus — women! Bah!' Reluctantly he moved away towards the kitchen.

Jerry glanced at the clock and noted that fifteen minutes had elapsed since his bride's departure. Gulping a little, but still game, he combed his hair, straight-ened his jacket, felt his chin to see if he needed a shave, and commenced to ascend the stairs.

The room was in darkness when he entered, but Angela's voice from the bed said, 'Put on the light, dear!'

He halted, momentarily stunned by her beauty as she smiled at him from the pillow. She stretched out her arms and Jerry sat on the bedside, holding her tightly to him.

Angela sighed. 'Hadn't you better — er — join me? It must be awfully cold sitting there.'

'Hmm! Er — yes — I mean — ' Jerry mumbled helplessly, then found his pajamas and switched off the light again.

He had removed his jacket only, when

through the slightly opened window came the sound of a revolver shot — and another, echoing faintly down to the village from the sinister castle on the hill!

For perhaps ten seconds Jerry stood paralyzed. Then he clicked on the light, his face tense. He said, 'Hartnell — at the castle! I'll have to go! The man may be in danger — '

'Oh, Jerry,' cried Angela. 'Please — please don't go up there. Something awful may happen. Please, for my sake . . . '

But Jerry scarcely heard her. If Hartnell was in a jam, Jerry wasn't the man to stand idly by and await results. Far from it. If he possibly could, he meant to have a hand in those results himself.

Quickly he donned his thick coat and picked up a poker from the fireplace and a torch from his case. He stopped briefly to kiss his distressed wife; then, with a sigh of 'What a honeymoon!', he was gone. And there was nothing Angela could do but wait . . .

Franz was in the lower room, staring through the window at the black outline of the castle on the hill. As Jerry rushed through, he turned and gasped, 'Where are you going?'

'Hartnell's in trouble,' Jerry told him. 'I'm going along to see if I can help.'

Then he was through the door, and Franz's voice came to him faintly: 'Mad! They are all mad, these English!'

Jerry didn't bother with the gate. By the aid of the rough irregularities in the stonework he shinned up the ten-foot wall, hung on the top for a moment, then dropped on the other side.

Running now, he found the narrow trail to Gräfshen Castle and raced along it, shining the torch before him to keep to the trail.

The castle was silent again now. Those three shots had been the only sound to come from the hill, and at the moment the place was so still and gloomy that they might have been nothing more than a figment of the imagination. Jerry wondered if they were — but no, Angela had heard them, and Franz.

He swung aside the creaking gate, and the squeal of the rust-ridden hinges set his nerves on edge.

Then he saw the figure — it came running towards him, tongue lolling out from a blank, idiotic face . . . Running without thought of where it was going . . . Its eyes were blank, staring pools of vacuity, and froth bubbled upon its lips.

It was hard to recognize the idiot for Hartnell — Henry Hartnell, the intelligent, scornful writer of things occult. But Hartnell it was; and without a sign or word he tore past Jerry, through the gates, out onto the cliff trail.

Jerry recovered from his astonishment, gripped his poker more tightly and looked for the horror which surely must be chasing Hartnell. He saw nothing; nothing but the withered trees; the lank, wet grass; the giant outlines of the castle itself.

He turned and ran after Hartnell, calling to him to stop.

Hartnell merely accelerated his pace. There was a bend in the trail ahead . . . Hartnell raced straight on, his unseeing eyes fixed on empty air . . . He ran right off the trail into space, over a sheer drop of two hundred feet, onto hard rock below.

Jerry groaned as Hartnell's flying figure

231

vanished from view. He ran to the edge of the rock and gazed down in horror. Nothing was visible down there, nor was anything audible. From first to last, Hartnell had made no sound, not even a moan.

Jerry found him there half an hour later, his neck cleanly broken. They carried him back to the village as dawn's light began to suffuse the mountains. Henry Hartnell had found at last that a revolver is no protection against the supernatural.

And on his neck, above his jugular, were two small tooth marks . . .

* * *

When Henry Hartnell had followed Count Elgin into the dark vastness of the castle, his mind had been functioning normally and clearly. True, there had been a hint of fear there, but he considered this only natural in the circumstances.

The Count had led him along a long passage into a musty-smelling, high-ceilinged room. 'The old dining hall,' supplied Count Elgin, lighting a large candelabra.

Hartnell found his fear overcome by his

curiosity, and gazed about him with interest. The furniture was draped in rotting dust sheets; the floor was carpeted by moss and lichen. On the high, dismal walls hung tattered portraits of the Counts of Gräfshen, too badly rotted to be recognizable.

In the centre of the room stood a long table which was uncovered. Upon this stood a bottle of rich red wine and two glasses. Count Elgin nodded him to a seat and said, 'You see, I am always prepared for company. Will you take a seat, Mr. Hartnell? Incidentally, am I correct in assuming you to be the writer on supernatural subjects?'

Hartnell nodded, accepting the glass of wine poured for him.

'I have read some of your works, Mr. Hartnell. Fascinating in the extreme. May I ask if they are your own opinions?'

'They weren't — until . . . '

'Until when?'

'Tonight.'

'Ah! So something has changed your views? I take it you now place more credence in ghouls and — vampires?'

Hartnell drained his wine, finding it stimulating and heady. He drew the gun from his pocket and laid it beside him on the table. He said, 'I am fully convinced, Count Gräfshen, that *you* are what is commonly known as a vampire!'

The Count smiled without humour. He said, 'Then weren't you rather foolish to come here? Aren't you afraid, Mr. Hartnell? Can't you feel worms of dread crawling up and down your spine?'

Hartnell laughed, not a very convincing laugh. 'I'm not afraid of you. Legend has it that a revolver is useless employed against a vampire. I am inclined to think otherwise. If the need arises I shall test the theory.'

Elgin smiled again. Hartnell felt a shudder run through him as he gazed into those burning, brilliant, evil eyes. Count Elgin said, 'I have no objection to you putting your theory to the test immediately. Would you care to do so?'

'What do you mean, Count Elgin?'

'Take your revolver in your hand. Go on, do as I say!'

Hartnell didn't wish to, but the power of the Count's eyes compelled him. Too late, he remembered that vampires were reputed to possess hypnotic powers. As if in a daze, he took up the gun.

'Level it at my heart — or where you would suppose my heart to be, assuming I had one,' said the Count with a smile.

Hartnell had to — the force of Count Elgin's glance was too strong to disobey his orders. He found himself sweating freely as he raised the gun and trained it upon the Count's immaculate evening dress.

'A charming chapter for your book — I shot a vampire!' said the Count. 'Unfortunately, I fear you will never write that book, Mr. Hartnell. Now fire!'

Hartnell's brain no longer had command of his movements. Some strange, unearthly force had entered into him, and although his own mind was still able to function and view the proceedings with a kind of numb horror, it was unable to resist the will of the Count. Hartnell pressed the trigger, and flame spurted from the muzzle. The Count did not move, although the bullet must have hit him directly through the heart.

'Try my forehead,' he told Hartnell.

Again the writer found himself controlled by some force which was utterly alien to him. The gun spat once more, and in Count Elgin's forehead appeared a neat, round hole. There was no blood.

'That is enough,' the Count told him. 'Understand, I would not permit everyone to take liberties with my person — but I am interested in convincing you, as a student of the occult, what a vampire's reactions are to revolver bullets. Nil, as you see.'

The hypnotic spell seemed to pass as the Count shifted his eyes from Hartnell's and the writer sank back weakly in his chair, exhausted by mental strain.

'Tell me,' he said. 'Miss Storm — the lady we found here last night. Did you — did you . . . ?'

'Attack her? Yes, I am responsible for the marks on her throat which, I presume, you could hardly have failed to notice.'

'And — is it true that whoever is bitten by a vampire will become one themselves?'

'No, Mr. Hartnell. That is utterly untrue — an exaggeration on the part of superstitious fools. Miss Storm is in no danger of becoming a vampire — but, may I add, she is absolutely under hypnotic control! If I care to exercise my powers, she will do just as I direct her — by means of mental telepathy.' He smiled and continued, 'A pity you will not be able to record this interview for posterity, is it not?'

Hartnell didn't want to think of the implication of his words. He forced himself to say, 'Have you the power of passing through solid substances? I refer to the door of the vault — it obviously hasn't been unlocked for centuries.'

'No, I have not that power. I gain access to the vault — where, during the hours of daylight, I must sleep — by means of a passage which runs from the castle. I find it more convenient that way.' He suddenly stiffened and rose. His lips curled back from his sharp, pointed teeth. He grated, 'And now, we have talked enough! You came up here to root out strange facts, I suppose? Well, you shall have one of the strangest experiences which could ever befall man. Look at me,

Mr. Hartnell . . . '

Hartnell looked; he couldn't help it. His wild eyes were drawn to the burning orbs of the Count. He felt them sinking into him, sinking into his soul, until the hall vanished, and he was floating upon a red mist, weird chords of sound clashing in his eardrums. Through it all, just above him, floated two brilliant pools of light — seeking, boring, subduing his impulses.

He felt the sharp prick at his throat; lay lazily while the strength appeared to drain from him . . . Then the redness began to fade, and cold horror clutched out for him. His hand went to his throat, felt the moist blood there . . . Count Elgin was at the opposite end of the table, laughing horribly. And suddenly, Hartnell's brain snapped! Uttering one shrill scream, he jumped from his chair and ran towards the passage by which he had entered.

Behind him, he knew, came Count Elgin; he chanced a look round as he reached the door and saw the vampire seeming to float silently behind him in mid-air. Then that weird force took control of him, and as he raced out into the night he knew that Count Elgin, and not he himself, was directing his steps!

Through the grounds he ran, pausing for nothing. Strive as he might, his mind, which still operated dazedly, could not drive out the evil will of the vampire. He remembered what the Count had said, about him not being able to record this experience. The Count meant to kill him — and that would be simple as long as he had Hartnell under his spell . . .

Dimly, Hartnell realized his flying feet were carrying him down the mountain trail; he seemed to hear a voice he knew shouting behind him . . . And with a feeling of sick terror, he knew he was approaching the bend in the pathway . . .

Hartnell made one last desperate attempt to regain control of his running body — but it was a feeble, hopeless effort. He saw the solid ground beneath his feet starting to turn; saw the blank space before him. And like a car out of control, he ran into space . . .

He was whirling, whirling round and round, over and over. It was icy cold, and though he tried to scream, he still could not direct his nerves. Then there was a jarring crash, a moment of fierce pain, and Henry Hartnell died . . .

# 6

## Netta Disappears

Jerry and Angela spent a mournful day at the inn following Hartnell's death. The dead writer had been carried by Jerry and Franz to the building that served as the village's police station, and Jerry had made a detailed statement to the officials.

Somehow, things seemed different. Now even Jerry believed in vampires, and later that evening, before sunset, he dragged himself away from his bride and went, not without a troubled mind, to Gräfshen Castle.

He, too, found the vault, and noted the rusty chains and bolts. Like Hartnell had done, he examined the exterior of the castle and noted the rear door, which appeared to have been in recent use. But at the moment it was locked from within.

Walking down the hill again, he came across Gail Storm, who was wandering through a sloping field on the right holding a small girl by the hand. Jerry recognized the child as Netta, the daughter of Franz and his fat wife. She was unlike her parents in every possible way: her hair was naturally curly and golden in hue, and her face was fresh-complexioned and happy. She was about ten or eleven, no more, and Jerry felt a twinge of pity that so innocent a child should be compelled to dwell in the shadow of Gräfshen Castle. When Gail Storm saw him, she released the little girl's hand, and Netta trotted off to gather some wild blossoms which grew nearby.

Jerry sat down on the ground in answer to Gail's invitation. He felt a little uncomfortable as the film star moved so close that their sides were almost touching, but he refrained from drawing away. She said, with a shuddering sigh, 'How terrible about poor Henry — Mr. Hartnell. He was such a gentleman.'

'A fine chap,' Jerry agreed, rather embarrassed. 'Pity he would insist on going up there . . . '

She sighed again and said, 'I — I

242

felt . . . safe, with him around. I can't describe it, but he seemed to give me a feeling of . . . security. Now it's gone. I'm all alone up here. No one who's interested in me to worry about me and protect me . . . '

Her large, liquid eyes looked directly at him, and Jerry flushed. He stammered awkwardly, 'Of course, I'd be only too happy to help if you are ever in trouble — as a fellow traveller, of course,' he added pointedly.

Gail smiled at him, her full red lips pouting a little. 'Of course, Mr. Liddon. What other interest could you have in me but that of a fellow journeyer? After all, you have a beautiful wife, have you not?'

She seemed to be deliberately taunting him; challenging his virtue. Not that Jerry had a great deal of virtue.

'Don't I interest you, Mr. — oh, that's silly! Suppose I just call you Jerry, and you call me Gail? Do you mind?'

'Not a bit, if it makes you happier.'

'I was saying — what was I saying? — oh, yes. Don't I interest you at all, Jerry?'

'Naturally, since you are a famous film actress. I'm always interested in personalities.'

'I didn't mean as a star. I meant, don't I interest you as . . . a woman?'

Jerry smiled. 'You've come a bit too late,' he said with brutal frankness. 'You might have done so once — and I won't say you wouldn't do so in, say, about another two years or so. But right now — well, to be candid, Gail, you don't interest me from a feminine angle at all.'

'I thought you said you would be willing to help me if ever the necessity arose?'

'By the same token I'd also be willing to help any woman! You understand — I make myself clear?'

'Yes — very clear, Mr. Liddon,' she said, dropping back to the formal manner of address again.

'Now, if there's nothing further, Miss Storm . . . ?'

She pouted suddenly and put out a detaining hand as he made to rise. She said, 'Oh, don't go! I don't really believe you aren't interested in me at all.'

'What makes you think that?'

'Perhaps it's my own conceit. Stay here a little while.'

'Look,' said Jerry wearily, 'I know you and your type. The best thing in trousers is what you like. If the best isn't available you'll take the next best for the time being. I'm no fool, Gail. And my conscience wouldn't permit me to flirt — oh, now don't get indignant! I know what you're driving at. You just have to have a man, isn't that it? Someone to pay you little attentions, and to tell you how cute you look, and all the rest of it. Well, you may as well get me right first time. I have a wife, whom I love — and whom I can trust. In return she trusts me, and I mean to justify that trust. So you see, how about that? Does it alter things?'

For answer she leaned forward unexpectedly, pressing her full red lips upon his tightly; pressing her supple, sensual body close to his. Even as he drew away, Jerry could not help thrilling to her softness and warmth. She said, looking at him from the corners of her eyes: 'How about *that*? Does *that* alter things?'

'It certainly does — it warns me to give you a wide berth in future!'

He saw the sudden look of anger in her face, and was amazed by it. It seemed that she was transformed from an over-sexed woman into a tigress — her eyes gleamed, her lip curled. She said, 'Very well — go back to your wife, my faithful friend. Perhaps you should have brought your mother along with you on the honeymoon, to take care of you!'

Jerry rose and said shortly, 'I should advise you to get back to the inn — it won't be so long to sunset now.' He turned and walked slowly to the village, leaving Gail calling for Netta.

He entered the inn and spoke to a harassed Franz who, at his wife's instigation, was busily dusting the lower room. 'Have you seen my wife anywhere?'

'She came in a short time ago. She seemed to be in a temper — went right up to her room, Mr. Liddon.'

Jerry wandered upstairs to their room. He tried the door and found it locked. He called, 'Angela — you there?'

From behind the door came a muffled

sob. Then she said, 'Go away, Jerry Liddon! I *hate* you!'

'Ye gods,' breathed Jerry to himself. 'Now what? What's wrong, dear?' he called. 'Have you hurt yourself?'

There was more sobbing. Then, 'No. You've hurt me, Jerry!'

'But how — what did I do?'

'Oh, you know well enough what you did! You told me you were going to look over the castle, didn't you? You wouldn't let me come — said it was too risky! And all the time you'd made a — a rendezvous with that — that woman! How could you, Jerry, on our honeymoon? I won't ever speak to you again!'

'But I didn't . . . ' spluttered Jerry.

'Don't lie to me — that only makes it worse! If you prefer that awful vamp to me, why don't you say so?'

'But I never . . . '

'Shut up! Don't you *dare* call me a liar! I was out walking round the village and saw you kissing her in a field!'

'Oh, so that's it. Well, Mrs. Liddon, for your information I wasn't kissing her; she was kissing me!' There was a renewed wail from within. 'Oh, hell!' said Jerry, realizing he had made matters worse. 'Come on, darling, don't be silly.'

'I'm silly now, am I? I *was* silly — silly to ever marry you! Go away, please! I don't want ever to see you again . . . oh — oh — oh!'

'Look, darling, open this door,' pleaded Jerry, 'and then I can explain everything.'

'Go away!'

'Will you please open this door!' roared Jerry, tearing his hair. 'You can be the most exasperating little . . . hem! I mean do open the door, dear — '

'You want me to?'

'Of course I do.'

'Very well.'

The door opened a few inches, and Jerry put on a winning smile. Unexpectedly a heavy boot appeared in his wife's hand, and wrapped itself lovingly about his head. The door shut again.

'Wow!' said Jerry. 'Why, I'll . . . '

He rattled the handle, but Angela made no further reply. Feeling angry with himself, Angela and Gail Storm, Jerry turned and retraced his steps towards the lower room. He meant to have a word with Gail, try to get her to explain to Angela that he had not fixed up an appointment. It was, at least, worth a try.

The sun had set, and the noise of the gates being locked came drifting in through the windows. Franz and his wife were in the hallway, jabbering like a pair of scalded hens, and as he came up to them the innkeeper grabbed his arm and babbled, 'You have been out? Tell me, did you see my little Netta? My poor little baby? This afternoon she goes out for a walk. I thought she had returned. She knows not to stray too far, and she is always back for sunset. But she is still missing. Perhaps you saw her?'

'Why, as a matter of fact I did. She was out in the fields with Miss Storm.'

'Miss Storm?'

A look of such fear crossed Franz's features that Jerry was afraid he would there and then have a stroke. His hands worked by his side and his lips twitched.

'Miss Storm?' he whispered again. 'The — woman who was bitten by — Count Elgin!'

'Oh, come now. She won't come to any harm. I feel sure she will be back any minute.'

As if to emphasize his words, there was a sudden knocking on the inn door. Franz, with a glad cry, hastened to open it. His wife stood mopping her tear-filled eyes.

Gail Storm walked in. But Netta was not with her.

'You,' hissed Franz. 'Where is my little girl? What have you done with her? Speak, or I will — kill you!'

Gail Storm turned her head towards him, and the look of cold fury in her eyes chilled Jerry and caused the innkeeper to shrink against the wall.

'I lost your child,' she said in a monotonous sing-song voice. 'She went to pluck flowers — I could not find her. She is still out there, for all I know!' She turned and walked mechanically to the stairs and up them. The three in the hall followed her with their eyes as she vanished from sight.

Then Franz gasped, 'I warned you — I warned you at first! She is evil! She is a

— a vampire, like Count Elgin! And now, where is my Netta? Why did you bring her here? Why, I ask you?' His eyes were rolling with alarm, and his accusing gaze was directed at Jerry, who stood awkwardly, crimsoning.

Finally, Jerry snapped, 'It isn't going to do any good hurling recriminations, Franz. She may be all right — must be all right! Best thing to do is to get out and look for her . . . now! Get your coat and come on — '

But Franz covered his eyes with his hands and moaned, 'It is too late. She is gone! My poor little Netta!'

'You mean you're too much of a coward to go out and look for your own child?' grunted Jerry, reaching for his own coat.

Franz made no reply, did not even look up. But his wife dried her eyes and nodded. 'That is what he means. He is afraid!'

'Then I'll damned well go by myself,' snapped Jerry, and without another glance at the cowering innkeeper he opened the door and stepped out.

There was a thin, melon-shaped slice of

moon riding high tonight. It didn't cast very much radiance, but it was sufficient for Jerry to see by. As he drew nearer the castle he could hear the fluttering of bats in the structure. Everything looked incredibly weird under the yellow radiance of that high moon. And close by the castle wall he found the limp little bundle . . .

He carried her back in his arms, walked into the inn with her and laid her on a settee. He said to the frantic parents, 'She is only bitten. She'll be all right.'

And, like a knell of doom in his ears, Franz gasped, 'Your wife — she went out with Miss Storm!'

# 7

## In the Vault

It was as if a gigantic hand had smashed into Jerry's very brain, numbing his faculties for a brief space of time — a second or two, during which he was suspended in an eternity of apprehension.

Then reason returned. Jerry said urgently, almost hysterically, 'What do you mean? Where did they go?'

Franz shook his head helplessly. He didn't know that. 'All I know is, while you were gone, they came walking down the stairs. They were both kind of stiff, unreal. They never spoke, but with Miss Storm leading went through the door. I watched them as far as the gate. That damned woman vampire opened it and they went out.'

'So that's how it came to be opened when I came back? But how could I have missed them?'

'That would not be hard — there are several ways to reach Gräfshen Castle from here.'

'You — you think they went to the castle?'

'But where else?'

Jerry didn't waste any more time answering. Once again he stumbled through the inn door and out of the gates. If he had been worried before, he was almost frantic now. Angela — gone, up there at the old castle, suffering God only knew what awful terrors. Terrors which had been enough to drive Hartnell, a strong man of the world, insane!

He redoubled his pace, trusting more to instinct than judgment to keep him on the pathway. And again the gaunt, grim castle loomed before him; again he threw open the rickety gate and entered the grounds.

Breathless, he came to the castle walls; went on round to the rear of the place. Then he saw Gail Storm — she looked ethereal, almost transparent in the pale moonshine. She stood motionless against the door in the rear of the castle and failed to observe Jerry, who had halted to consider his next move.

Without warning she turned, bent slightly and walked stiffly into the opening behind her. It was as if she had heard some mental call — some order, issued by means of telepathy. She neglected to close the small door and Jerry, his breath hissing from between his teeth, followed her into the darkness.

A musty smell was in his nose; the dampness was almost a tangible substance in the air. His feet slid upon growths of ancient fungus, but he retained his balance.

He came to the big hall and saw the candelabra which held three glimmering candles. He paused again to take stock.

Count Elgin was there, and Gail, and — Angela!

She was standing by the table, clad only in a flimsy robe; her eyes were glazed, staring fixedly into space, her features immobile. Jerry knew at a glance that she was in a trance of some description.

Count Elgin was moving a small stone ornament set in an alcove in the wall. In answer to his touch, a square section of the solid stone slid aside, and the Count turned to his companions. To Gail he said, 'You have followed my directions well, my dear! Tonight you have brought me two victims, the child and this woman. I shall retain this woman here; her husband will probably — almost certainly — come to seek her. And then I will secure a further victim! It would be unwise for you to return to the inn, so I think that you had better rest in the vaults with me. Come.'

His eyes bored into the two girls, and automatically they both moved towards the opening.

Jerry felt that wave of fear again, and a feeling that if Angela entered that dark tunnel he would never see her again.

With a hoarse shout he broke into the open, and Count Elgin spun about to face him. Red, flame-like eyes burnt into Jerry's skull; icy tremors chased along his spine. He seemed to be floating in a red mist, floating in a void through which those ages-old eyes stared stonily at him . . .

Another moment and — but the moment did not come! With a mighty effort of will Jerry forced his mind back from the dark paths it was taking. Insistently he repeated to himself that he did not believe in vampires; he did not believe in the Count, nor his hypnotic powers ... and gradually the room crystallized before him.

The Count was still there, but now his eyes were directed elsewhere. Obviously he thought Jerry was already in his power, and was deliberating what he should do.

Jerry knew that to move, to betray his awareness, would be to invite the glare of those eyes again, and wisely he remained motionless, staring glassily in front of him. He knew that if the Count subjected him to a second ordeal he would never have the strength to resist it.

It was all clear to him now: Gail Storm, under the Count's control, had brought him his victims, Netta, and Angela. Probably she had, through the Count, hypnotized Jerry's wife and led her up here. Certainly Angela would not have gone with her of her own free will.

Jerry came back with a jerk and realized that the two girls were proceeding down the tunnel, and that the Count was looking towards him frowningly. He realized that the Count had issued some mental order to him. Unless he obeyed it, Elgin would realize that he was not under control.

There was only one order which might have been issued, and Jerry took the chance. Stiffly, jerkily, he moved towards the passage, stooped and entered it.

The frown left the Count's face, and he followed the others. Jerry noted how he closed the hidden entrance, then hastily crept onwards. The Count, carrying the candelabra, came behind.

They walked for about five minutes, then emerged into a high, gloomy, corrupt-smelling vault. The Gräfshen resting place.

Coffins, beset by wood-rot, lay indiscriminately about the stone shelves. Cobwebs, alive with spiders, festooned the corners and angles. In the far corner, unreached by the light, a company of rats squealed a macabre dirge.

Jerry shivered as he felt insects

squashing beneath his feet; bats fluttered haphazardly, blindly, about the tomb in the sudden glare of light . . . Vampire bats, bloodsuckers, smaller editions of the Count himself!

The Count laid his candelabra aside and Jerry, as if obeying his unspoken command, moved over with the two girls to a corner of the vault.

Here the girls lay down, passively, in the filth and rot; and Jerry was quick to follow their example, though not without a feeling of loathing.

Then Count Elgin came across and stood looking down upon him. 'Hmm!' he muttered to himself. 'My larder is certainly well replenished — and now that I have secured the English people, there is no one in the village with courage to disturb me, or attempt to trace them! I shall dine well tonight!' A ghastly, obscene chuckle fluttered from his red maw. He stooped and knelt beside Jerry. And Jerry, with a thrill of disgust, knew that he was going to dine — off him!

It was mental and physical torture to lay still while the gruesome undead thing fed from his throat; but Jerry dare not reveal that he was in possession of his senses — it would have been fatal. So he was forced to endure the attentions of the Count; forced to lie there limply while the foul creature pierced his throat and drank of his blood. His nocturnal thirst sated, Count Elgin rose and crossed the chamber. Jerry breathed a relieved sigh when he saw the Count was satisfied — that he would not bother Angela, at least for now.

The Count sat on a coffin by the candelabra, picked up a large, musty volume from the floor, and began flicking the leaves over. It was indeed a strange experience, lying there motionless while an actual vampire read from an ancient volume. Now and again Jerry stole a glance at his wrist watch; and when the fingers finally pointed to four thirty, he could have cheered with joy. For he knew that, according to legend, at dawn the vampire must retire to rest in his own coffin, over earth in which he had been buried.

And Count Elgin Gräfshen was not an

exception! Some inner sense seemed to tell the Count when it was dawn; he glanced at his prisoners and, apparently satisfied by their appearance of coma, he went to the vault door and inspected the chains which secured the inside to see that they were quite safe.

He returned, raised the lid of the leaden coffin on which he had been seated, and carefully lowered himself into the box. The lid closed. On the inside, a bolt was shot home. Count Gräfshen took no chances of being disturbed but, thought Jerry, grimly, this was time when he was *going* to be disturbed — very definitely so, and then some.

As the bolt was shot home, Jerry raised a hand to his sore throat and rubbed the two incisions there. Then he rose and softly tried to awaken Angela and Gail Storm. He might as well have saved his energies. They were quite insensible to anything.

He wondered, with momentary panic, if they would ever snap out of it. Sternly he drove these thoughts aside.

He knew what he must do, at once. The

vampire legends said the only way to kill a vampire was to drive a heavy wooden stake through its heart as it lay in its coffin. There were plenty of wooden stakes here! But he had to find a means of opening the coffin first.

Rapidly he made his way back along the secret passage, into the dining room. Early-morning sunlight was streaking in through the broken, grime-shrouded windows. By its aid he found what he sought: a stout, heavy steel sword.

He hastened back to the charnel room and crossed to the casket. It was almost more than he could do to raise the coffin on its side, but with the help of the sword he managed it. He inserted the flat blade between crack of lid and coffin wall and tried to lever the lid open. He found a heavy stone and hammered savagely upon the hilt of the weapon with this. Gradually the blade penetrated, and with a final immense wrench the lid snapped from its hinges.

Jerry lowered the coffin lid flat again; he had no wish to tip out the villainous monster within. He raised the lid.

And started back, a cry of horror springing to his lips.

Count Elgin Gräfshen lay there, eyes open, malevolent, staring fixedly above him! He was conscious, but unable to move; powerless to raise a finger in his defence. The rising sun had robbed him of his strength, and now he knew the fate which awaited him, and could do nothing to avert it!

For long minutes Jerry stood frozen; stood, taking care to keep out of range of those magnetic eyes.

Then like a man in a dream, or nightmare, he began to seek about the tomb for a long, sharp wooden stake. In the fading light of the candles he found one — the remains of a broken-down oak casket. It was about three inches thick and two feet long. Holding it tightly, with sudden determination, he approached the staring, helpless creature in the casket.

He placed the stake directly above the vampire's heart and raised the heavy stone he had been using. And, with the full force of his little body, he crashed it down upon the blunt end of the stake. It penetrated keenly, and Jerry continued hammering.

Count Elgin's features were dreadful to watch. At the bite of the sharp wood his lips twisted and curved back from his teeth in a paroxysm of agony. His fiery eyes burned with pain, and Jerry could almost imagine him inwardly shrieking. But his pallid face stayed in the one position on the plush lining of his casket; his gaunt body did not move one inch.

It was long minutes before the Count's writhing flesh relaxed. Jerry watched as the crimson hue faded from his lips; as his already pale face assumed the texture of wax; and as his eyelids closed tiredly over his now-dull eyes.

The Vampire of Gräfshen Castle was no more, if legend spoke truly.

And with his passing, as if awakening from a deep sleep, Angela and Gail stretched their arms and gazed about them. The hypnotic trance was broken; they were free from the clutches of Count Elgin's unholy mind.

Jerry hurried to bustle them from the scene before they were fully aware of where they were — and what that implied.

Outside the sun was shining; birds were singing in the castle grounds, where before only bats and owls had held court. Already, it seemed to Jerry, the trees were taking on fresh life.

He explained as much as he thought they should hear as they went down the hill towards the village. It was hard to explain to Gail Storm, who recalled nothing since her first meeting with the Count after the accident. But by the time they reached Safnia the girls fully understood everything.

Leaving them with Franz and his wife, Jerry set off grimly for the police station. It was his duty to report what had happened at the castle.

# 8

## Honeymoon's End

Jerry did not return until the next morning. Angela had somehow managed to get to sleep the previous night — a sleep born of utter exhaustion — but she had been up early, and was anxiously awaiting his return at the door of the inn. She ran out and threw her arms around him.

'Oh, Jerry, I've been so worried! They — they haven't charged you with murder, have they?'

Jerry gently disengaged himself from his wife's embrace and held her at arm's length. 'They could hardly do that, dear! When I took them back to the castle to show them the Count's corpse — *there wasn't one!* Just a pile of dust and bones mouldering in the coffin. It seems that nearly three hundred years suddenly caught up with him! So — no corpse, no murder charge. Not,' Jerry reflected, 'that there was ever any danger of that, even if the body *had* remained intact. Everyone in the village knows I only acted in self-defence.'

As they went into the inn, Jerry added: 'But there was another development at the station.' He broke off, smiling at Angela's anxious expression. 'It concerns Hartnell, dear. You'll remember I took his body in to the station earlier? They've a telephone there — one of the very few in the village. Well, I managed to remember the name of his English publishers, so I asked them to get in touch, so the publisher could notify his relatives. That was the least I could do, for the memory of a brave man.

'When we got back from the castle last night, I learned that the publishers had been asking to speak to me. I returned their call and spoke to their editor, who told me that Hartnell had a contract for another book about his experiences in Safnia. They wanted to hire me to complete it — to tell the story of how Hartnell met his tragic end. They reckon it will be a bestseller!' Angela frowned, and Jerry added hastily: 'Naturally, I'll share the royalties with his relatives.'

'That's not what's worrying me, dear. It's just that — well, you're an engineer, not an author. You've never written anything, so how — ?'

Jerry laughed. 'The publisher will take care of that — they're going to provide me with a ghost writer.'

Angela gave a little shudder. 'Just so long as he's not a *real* ghost . . . '

\* \* \*

'So you see,' said Jerry, 'I don't want to say I told you so . . . '

'No, dear,' said Angela meekly.

'So I won't say it,' continued Jerry magnanimously. 'But I was against the idea of spending our honeymoon in Safnia all along.'

'Yes, dear,' said Angela contritely.

'And what a honeymoon it's been!' Jerry concluded. 'What with a sinister old castle, a film star, a murdered writer, and a vampire, I don't know whether I'm on my head or my heels.'

It was the following day, and they were busy packing. Angela had explained how Gail Storm had knocked at her door on that fateful evening, persuading her to open it by telling her Jerry had run into trouble at the castle. From there on, with the Count's hypnotic powers behind her, it had been easy to put the influence on Angela.

They completed their packing. Jerry had announced his intention of leaving at once, and Angela had meekly agreed. There was no romance left in Safnia for her, after what had happened.

But the village itself was happy again — no longer a village of fear! The happy laughter of children rang out from every side. They frolicked in the square, on the hill path, even in the old castle grounds itself.

The menfolk had half-heartedly accompanied Jerry on a return journey to the vault, and had seen for themselves the disintegrated remains of what had once been Count Elgin Gräfshen — 1635–1946! They had rejoiced, and heaped thanks upon the cause of their rejoicing. But Jerry was adamant in his decision to leave the village; even now, when he looked at the castle, he could not repress a feeling of nervous tension.

Franz, Netta gamboling happily by his side, escorted them and Gail Storm to the door. The coach from Iswaldia was calling that day, with a fresh consignment of passengers — and when it returned to Iswaldia, Jerry, Angela and Gail intended to be aboard it.

Franz was really regretful to see them go; he refused to take what they owed him, and assured them that if at any time they wished to return to Safnia, they were welcome at his humble inn.

The shouts of the children announced the arrival of the coach; as usual, the driver was anxious to get away from Safnia as soon as possible. He unloaded his passengers as rapidly as he could: two maiden ladies, school teachers, on holiday. They were thrilled with the old-world charm of Safnia, and spoke warmly of the various sights.

'Oh, do look, Esmerelda,' said one, 'at

that quaint old tavern!'

'And they've got a well, Lucy, dear,' cooed her companion.

'And a little funny old church . . . '

'And queer cobbled streets . . . '

'And whatever is that old wall built round the place for?'

'That, Madam,' interrupted Jerry coldly, 'is to keep out the vampires!'

'The what?' said the two old souls in horror.

'Vampires,' reiterated Jerry. 'You know, the things which leave their coffins at night and prowl about sucking blood from human victims.'

'Rubbish!' snapped Lucy. 'Are you trying to be clever, young man? Do you think we are fools?' She threw her nose in the air, and the two old dames walked off haughtily.

Smiling, Jerry and his two companions piled into the carriage. The contraption rumbled away, the horses making hard going up the hill. Slowly the grim outline of Gräfshen castle died from their view, and Jerry sat back with a sigh.

It was when they were nearing Iswaldia

that the driver said, 'So you're not staying at Safnia? Perhaps the vampire frightened you, eh?'

'Perhaps it did,' admitted Jerry.

'Well, we have a fine hotel in Iswaldia — perhaps you will stay there?'

'Perhaps we will,' agreed Jerry. 'How about it, Angela?'

'Might as well start our real honeymoon there as anywhere!'

They had no difficulty in obtaining rooms, and as the driver had said, the hotel was, if not modern, at least comfortable.

Jerry, leaving Angela to unpack her things, drifted down to the public bar and listened to the scraps of conversation there. He spoke the language fairly well, for Angela had been teaching him.

A whiskery character in a beer-mottled suit was saying, 'Aye! They brought the poor girl in this morning — she had two teeth marks on her neck!'

'But,' gasped a second, 'there has never been a vampire in or around Iswaldia!'

'No — but there's got to be a first time, hasn't there? And this is the second in two nights . . .'

A sudden blur flashed past them, and they stared up. The old man said, 'That's the Englishman who's staying here — they're all mad, Englishmen!'

Jerry burst into the room where Angela was still unpacking, and started slinging his things hastily into his case again.

'Why — what — ' stammered Angela. 'Jerry! I thought we were staying here? How about our honeymoon?'

'To hell with our honeymoon — we're going to sit at the station and catch the first train out of here . . . if it takes us all night!'

## THE END

We do hope that you have enjoyed reading this large print book.

Did you know that all of our titles are available for purchase?

We publish a wide range of high quality large print books including:
**Romances, Mysteries, Classics**
**General Fiction**
**Non Fiction and Westerns**

Special interest titles available in large print are:
**The Little Oxford Dictionary**
**Music Book, Song Book**
**Hymn Book, Service Book**

Also available from us courtesy of Oxford University Press:
**Young Readers' Dictionary**
**(large print edition)**
**Young Readers' Thesaurus**
**(large print edition)**

For further information or a free brochure, please contact us at:
**Ulverscroft Large Print Books Ltd.,**
**The Green, Bradgate Road, Anstey,**
**Leicester, LE7 7FU, England.**
**Tel:** (00 44) 0116 236 4325
**Fax:** (00 44) 0116 234 0205

*Other titles in the*
*Linford Mystery Library:*

# THE DOCTOR'S DAUGHTER

## Sally Quilford

Whilst the Great War rages in Europe, sleepy Midchester is pitched into a mystery when a man is found dead in an abandoned house. Twenty-four-year-old Peg Bradbourne is well on the way to becoming a spinster detective, but it is a role she is reluctant to accept. When her stepmother also dies in suspicious circumstances, Peg makes a promise to her younger sister, putting aside her own misgivings in order to find out the truth.

# SERGEANT CRUSOE

## Leslie Wilkie

Luke Sharp is unaware that he has a double — Marco Da Silva, the ruthless criminal gang leader known as 'Silver'. When a pair of vigilantes intent on taking their revenge against Silver shoot Luke by mistake, his life is changed dramatically. Convalescing at his grandfather's home, he agrees to transcribe the old man's wartime memoirs of his exploits in the South Pacific. However, Silver finds out about Luke, and attempts to coerce him into work as his double in crime . . .

# HOUSE OF FOOLS

## V. J. Banis

Toby Stewart has been invited by her sister Anne to visit her at Fool's End, the manor where she works as a personal secretary to a famous author, and after his recent death has stayed on to catalogue his papers and manuscripts. But on arriving, Toby is dismayed to learn that Anne has mysteriously disappeared — without taking any of her possessions and without informing her employers. And most everyone there, it seems, has something to hide. Did Anne leave of her own volition — or has she perhaps been murdered . . . ?

# DEATH VISITS KEMPSHOTT HOUSE

## Katherine Hutton

Nick Shaw, travel writer and enthusiastic archer, expects to spend an enjoyable weekend with his partner, Louisa, at the luxurious Kempshott House Hotel. Then a body is discovered during an archery club contest on the hotel's grounds, stuck through with three arrows. The police are called in, assisted by Louisa — a detective sergeant — and it soon becomes apparent that the man has been deliberately murdered. Worse still, it would appear that the murderer hasn't finished yet . . .